school Statue SHOWDOWN

David Starr

James Lorimer & Company Ltd., Publishers
Toronto

James Lorimer & Company Ltd., Publishers acknowledges funding support from the Ontario Arts Council (OAC), an agency of the Government of Ontario. We acknowledge the support of the Canada Council for the Arts. This project has been made possible in part by the Government of Canada and with the support of Ontario Creates.

Cover design: Tyler Cleroux
Cover illustrations: Kate Phillips, Shutterstock,

Library and Archives Canada Cataloguing in Publication

Title: School statue showdown / David Starr.
Names: Starr, David (School principal), author.
Identifiers: Canadiana (print) 20230229050 | Canadiana (ebook) 20230229069
   |ISBN 9781459417557 (hardcover) | ISBN 9781459417540 (softcover)
   | ISBN 9781459417564 (EPUB)
Classification: LCC PS8637.T365 S36 2023 | DDC jC813/.6—dc23

Published by:
James Lorimer & Company
Ltd., Publishers
117 Peter Street, Suite 304
Toronto, ON, Canada
M5V 0M3
www.lorimer.ca

Distributed in Canada by:
Formac Lorimer Books
5502 Atlantic Street
Halifax, NS, Canada
B3H 1G4
www.formaclorimerbooks.ca

Distributed in the US by:
Lerner Publisher Services
241 1st Ave. N.
Minneapolis, MN, USA
55401
www.lernerbooks.com

Printed and bound in Canada.

For Ronald Hatch
and for the nephews

MoNDay

Alex Sullivan Junior, or AJ, as everyone in the town of Big River knew him, was in a great mood. School was over for the day, the late-March sun was warm overhead, the snow was almost gone, and baseball was starting in a month. To get ready for the season, AJ, Jackson Thomas, and Steve Pearson were throwing a ball on the school's field, even though some small piles of dirty snow remained.

"Great toss, Jackson," said AJ. Jackson played first base. He almost never missed a pass and had the strongest arm on the team. AJ was the catcher, and the two of them had combined to get a lot of outs last season.

"Not bad," Steve added. Steve played left field. He wasn't the greatest baseball player — hockey was his game — but he played because AJ, his oldest friend, did. All three boys were on the local baseball team, the Big River Foresters.

They wore red and blue with a pair of crossed hatchets as the logo. The meaning of the hatchets was obvious, and though nobody was quite certain how red and blue had become Big River colours, Mr. Corbett, the school's Social Studies teacher, said they were chosen because that was what was on the Canadian flag before the Maple Leaf was chosen. But whatever the reason, AJ and the rest of the kids who played sports in town wore them proudly.

"Want to practice again tomorrow after school?" AJ asked later when they were leaving the field.

"Works for me," said Steve.

"I can't," Jackson said. "Dad let me take the truck today, but I have to ride the bus tomorrow. Besides, there's some stuff going on back home."

AJ and Steve lived in town, but Jackson lived on the Big River First Nation, about half an hour north. The bus left not long after classes ended, so Big River kids who had to take the bus couldn't stay for after-school activities unless they got their own ride home.

"Stuff? Are you okay?" asked AJ. He'd known Jackson for years. He seemed a little distant.

"It's all good," Jackson said. "Don't worry about it."

"If you say so," AJ said, though he could tell something was up with Jackson. His friend looked downright uncomfortable.

On his way to the parking lot, AJ patted the shoulder of the statue that stood by the front doors of the school, just as he did every day. The statue was of Harold Sullivan, the school's namesake — and AJ's great-grandfather. It was a life-size wooden copy of the photo that hung on the wall of AJ's living room. In that picture Harold Sullivan stood proudly, a smile on his face, a logger's hatchet in his hand.

Harold Sullivan Secondary School. How many kids could attend a school named after their relative? And then there was the statue. No matter how many times he saw the statue, AJ always found it a little weird just how much he looked like his great-grandfather. It was almost as if AJ was looking at an older, wooden version of himself. On the base of the statue was the dedication to Harold. *In Honour of Harold Sullivan, January 16, 1885–June 25, 1973. Hard Work, Integrity, Family, Community.* Those five words described Harold and had become the family motto. AJ had known those words all his life.

'Hatchet' Harold Sullivan was a legend in Big River, after all. The most successful Sullivan in a line going back 150 years, back to the time when the town was nothing more than a fur trading post in the middle of the wilderness. Big River had grown a lot since those early days, thanks in large part to his great-grandfather. Harold was a war hero, serving his country in both the First and the Second World Wars. He was a businessman, a politician, and a benefactor. It was said that Harold built the modern town of Big River almost by himself, carving it out of the wilderness tree by tree with his trademark axe.

AJ was proud to be a Sullivan, especially these days. On the fiftieth anniversary of Harold's death, Alex Sullivan Senior, AJ's dad and the owner of Sullivan Sawmills, the biggest company in town, had announced that the mill would be funding a new twenty-thousand-dollar scholarship in honour of Harold, to be given each year to the student who best

7

exemplified the characteristics Harold stood for. It was the largest scholarship in the history of the school.

AJ hopped into his pickup, fired up the engine, and drove out of the parking lot toward home. The Ford half-ton wasn't new, not by a longshot, but AJ was proud of it. He'd paid for the truck himself. He'd saved for a year to buy it, working weekend and holiday shifts at the family mill. AJ's dad had offered to loan him the money for the truck, but AJ wanted to buy it himself. The Sullivans were hard-working, independent people, and AJ wasn't about to take a handout, even from his own father.

Big River may have grown up over the years, but it was still a small town. Barely five thousand people called it home, but AJ couldn't imagine living anywhere else. After all, he could get almost everything he needed here. There were stores, a baseball diamond, a hockey rink, a curling club, and even a small movie theatre. If there was something AJ or his family wanted that Big River couldn't provide, then it was only a couple hours' drive south to the city.

The city. Why would anyone want to live down there? Too many people, too much noise, too many lights. The city was fine if they needed to buy equipment for the mill or go and watch a professional hockey game, but that was about it.

Who on earth would trade this for concrete and traffic jams and tiny apartments? thought AJ.

Big River might be small, and the winters might be long, but the town had been perfect for the seven generations of Sullivans who had come before him, and it was perfect for AJ as well.

As AJ drove, he looked over to the river that had lent the town its name. The water ran high with the spring melt, churning white and green. On the banks, the cottonwood and birch trees were budding. Overhead the sky was a bright blue, and the cool spring air was fresh and clean.

AJ quickly left the town behind him, travelling north toward home. The pavement would end in another ten kilometres, stopping at Sullivan Sawmills, but the road carried on another thirty kilometres to the Big River First Nation. AJ slowed down and turned onto a long gravel driveway, through an open gate, and toward the Home Ranch.

His family had lived at the Home Ranch for nearly one hundred years, in a large log house on a benched slope overlooking the Big River and its valley. The Home Ranch was only a half section, 130 hectares of land, and not large at all compared to some of the other ranches in the area, but it was beautiful. And it wasn't as if the place was a working ranch anymore. AJ's father was too busy running the mill and the other family businesses to ranch, and a couple of horses and a few dozen head of cattle were enough for his mom, Linda, to look after.

AJ's mom had grown up on a ranch south of town, a massive two sections of land with three hundred head of cattle, and she'd taught her son everything she knew about ranching. Thanks to her, AJ could talk about steers and growing hay and wrangling horses with a knowledge appreciated by the most experienced ranchers in Big River, and because of the mill and his dad, he knew about logging and milling as well.

When AJ pulled up to the house, he was surprised to see his dad's pickup parked next to his mom's SUV. It was only four-thirty. His dad usually stayed at the mill until five, making sure that everything was good to go for the second shift to start work.

"I'm home. Is everything okay?" asked AJ when he kicked off his boots and walked into the kitchen.

His parents were sitting at their large pine table. His father had his iPad in his hands. He was reading the website of the town's newspaper, the *Big River Gazette*, and AJ could see that his dad was furious. His father wore his emotions on his sleeve at the best of times.

"No, son, it isn't," said his dad. "I don't suppose you read the paper today?"

"You're kidding, right?" said AJ. He rarely read the local paper, in print or online. It was little more than ads for businesses, small-town gossip, and local interest stories.

His dad passed AJ the tablet. "You need to read it today. Look at this."

"Big River First Nation demand name change of Big River High School."

"Is this a joke?" AJ asked after he read the bold letters of the headline.

"No joke. Keep reading. Aloud."

"Big River First Nations have made public their demand that the Big River School district rename Harold Sullivan High School and remove the statue from the grounds. When asked why, Big River First Nation Chief Robert Thomas claimed that the 'recent announcement by the Sullivan family to name their new scholarship after Harold Sullivan shows that the community in general and the Sullivan family in particular, do not understand Sullivan's racist past. In an age of reconciliation, it's well past time this town recognized the role that Harold Sullivan played in the injustice directed against our ancestors.'"

"What is he talking about?" AJ asked. "Racist? Injustice? What do they have against Great-Grandpa Harold?"

"Keep reading," his dad said. "It's not just Harold they're attacking."

AJ continued. "Sullivan discriminated against First Nations people. He profited from stolen reservation land and was actively involved in sending Big River First Nation children to the Sturgeon Lake Residential School, many of whom did not return to their local reserve. Big River First Nation feels that now is the time for our people to take this stand. After all, Sullivan, along with other so-called town fathers like Robert Pearson, was a driving force in sending our children to residential school. As mayor, he drafted racist and exclusionary policies against our people. Not only that, but he was also personally responsible for the destruction of the Freedom Camp, one of the darkest chapters in the history of Big River First Nation. Fifty years after Sullivan's passing, these are the things that need to be remembered and acknowledged and we will do so by presenting this petition to the chair of the school board at next Monday's School Board Meeting."

"It's garbage," AJ's dad said. "My grandfather may have died when I was a baby, but I grew up knowing everything about him, and I can tell you one hundred percent that this is not true. Harold built this town, and he was a good man, a family man. Can you believe the nerve of these people? Two weeks before we commemorate the life of the most important figure in this town's history, and Robert pulls this crap?"

"I know, Alex," began AJ's mom in a soothing voice. "I think the name of the school and the statue should stay, and I disagree with what Robert said about the family. It's not right to disrupt the celebration and appear ungrateful about the scholarship, but Harold was known to hold certain views. Don't forget that people from the Big River First Nation weren't exactly welcome in town and that their kids weren't even allowed to attend the school until after Harold died."

"Everyone held certain views back then," AJ's dad snapped. "That was how things were in his time. I'm not denying that, but it was the government that made those kids go to residential school, not my grandfather. Robert is practically saying Harold killed those kids himself and now it's our fault! Harold stood for hard work, integrity, family, and community. All of us Sullivans do, and there's no way I'm going to let Robert trash our name."

"What was the Freedom Camp?" AJ asked. He'd heard the family motto a thousand times but had never heard of Freedom Camp.

"When Harold was first elected mayor not long after the war ended, he had some houses that a few Native war veterans built on the outskirts of town burned down," his mom explained. "They called it Freedom Camp. I haven't heard that name since I was a little girl. I'd almost forgotten about it."

"Freedom Camp," scoffed his dad. "What a joke. They were a handful of squatter houses built on town land without permits. They were a fire hazard, and Harold was only upholding the law. That was his job. He was the mayor and was elected to do just that. Besides, it's ancient history now and has nothing to do with us."

"Jackson's dad, of all people," said AJ, getting as worked up as his father. AJ felt as if his friend and his family had just slapped him across the face. Right after they'd spent an hour playing catch together.

Stuff going on back home, Jackson had said. *This sort of stuff,* AJ guessed. Jackson had to have known all about the petition but hadn't said a thing. No wonder he seemed nervous.

Then his dad's phone rang. "Hey, Buck," he said. AJ knew who was calling. Buck Pearson, Steve's dad, was one of his dad's oldest friends. Buck Pearson was a big fourth-generation logging contractor in town — and Robert Pearson's grandson. The Pearsons had been in Big River almost as long as the Sullivans. "Yeah, I'm reading it right now. Unbelievable, right? You bet we're gonna be doing something about this." They talked for a few more seconds, then AJ's father hung up.

"Robert Thomas seems to have forgotten that his logging company gets most of his business from me," he said. "Though not for long. He's not going to make one more dollar from the Sullivans, and I'll make certain that nobody else hires him either. That's the price he's going to pay for disrespecting our family. This is just the beginning, son, you mark my words. If Robert Thomas wants a fight, he's going to get one."

TUESDAY

AJ could see that something was wrong the moment he parked his truck at school. And he wasn't the only one. A large crowd of students and teachers were gathered outside the front doors, a crowd that got bigger when a school bus pulled up. Many of the kids who attended Sullivan High School lived out of town, on ranches and farms throughout the valley and they bussed to school, as did the kids who lived out at Big River First Nation. AJ watched as the Big River First Nation bus arrived, the fifty or so students now joining the pack, though their reactions to what they were seeing seemed to be different than those of the kids from town.

The statue of Harold Sullivan, his own great-grandfather had been vandalized. Someone had covered it with orange paint. Not put on with a brush or roller, but as if an entire can had been splashed on Harold and the sidewalk around him.

14

"I can't believe this," said Steve when he spotted AJ approaching.

Neither could AJ when he saw what had happened. Orange paint. AJ understood the significance. Orange was the colour used to remember kids who went to residential schools. AJ had worn an orange shirt himself on Orange Shirt Day. He knew what it meant and knew it was no coincidence, not after that awful story in the Gazette yesterday.

AJ saw Jackson Thomas in the crowd. While his friend looked as surprised at the damage as everyone else, he sure didn't seem to be very upset about it. Jackson returned AJ's look and shrugged as if to say *I didn't do it,* but all AJ could think about were the terrible things Jackson's dad had said about Harold, and despite being friends with Jackson and growing up together, AJ felt a wave of anger roll over him. It didn't help that many of the Big River First Nation students were taking pictures of the defaced statue. Some were smiling and a few were even laughing.

"Okay, okay, let's break it up. The bell's about to ring." Ms. Shorthouse, the principal, was now outside, along with several of the teachers. Reluctantly the students started to move, walking slowly toward their classes.

"I bet you Jackson knows who did this," said Steve. "He may have even done it himself."

"Maybe," replied AJ, but he didn't really believe it. He'd known Jackson for years and had even gone out to his house on the First Nation, which wasn't something a lot of the kids from town could say. "But I just can't see him doing it."

"Too bad the school doesn't have security cameras," said Steve.

"Yeah. Too bad." With the rare exception of an occasional broken window and graffiti tags, the school was never vandalized. Harold Sullivan High School didn't need security cameras. Such things were for big city problems that just didn't happen in Big River. Until now.

As the day went along social media lit up. AJ had accounts on Instagram, Discord, and Snapchat, and photos and messages were flying all over the place. There were lots of comments from people who were upset about what had happened to the statue, but there were also quite a few that justified the vandalism. Not just people in town, either. Somehow the damage done to Harold's statue had gone province-wide. AJ couldn't understand why there were so many people, people who didn't even know Harold, who seemed ready to believe the very worst things about his great-grandfather, and the comments made him angry.

At lunchtime, AJ went outside. Mr. Peterson, the school custodian, had done a good job cleaning the paint off the statue. Most of it was gone but there were still streaks of orange on the concrete, and in the wooden nooks and furrows of the statue some paint remained. AJ also saw an RCMP vehicle in the school parking lot. He was glad about that. No doubt Ms. Shorthouse had called the detachment to report the vandalism. AJ hoped that the police would take it seriously and arrest those responsible.

A strange tension had settled over the school. Big River was a small town and all the kids, those from town as well as those from the First Nation, had known each other for years, but today students gathered in small groups, looking at each other with suspicion. After lunch AJ went back to class and when the day ended, he headed straight for his truck. Normally AJ would hang out with friends or do his homework, but today he felt drained, and the last thing he wanted to do was stay at school.

Then AJ saw Jackson and some of the other Big River First Nation students waiting for their bus. He hadn't planned on saying anything, but suddenly AJ found himself heading toward the bus loop instead of his truck.

"Why is your dad doing this, Jackson?" AJ asked.

Jackson looked uncomfortable. "I'm sorry, AJ, but my dad is right."

"*Right?* You think spreading lies and insulting my family is right?"

"They aren't lies!" Jackson snapped. "What my dad said is the truth. Harold Sullivan was a racist."

"That's garbage! You take it back!"

But Jackson didn't look like he was about to back down. A crowd grew around the boys. Tommy, David, and Charlie, three Big River First Nation students stood near Jackson while Steve and a handful of boys from town came up to AJ.

"You have something to say about my family, too, Jackson?" Steve snarled. "We can talk if you want. Off school grounds." Everyone knew what that meant. Steve was hotheaded and had been suspended for *talking* to somebody off school grounds last year. The crowd buzzed.

"Fine," Jackson said, his face flushed with anger.

The crowd continued to grow. The Big River First Nation school bus arrived but none of the students climbed on. Then Mr. Corbett appeared. "Jackson get on the bus. The rest of you, go home," he said. "This isn't going to help things." Nobody moved. "Now," Mr. Corbett ordered.

"You tell your dad to stop it," AJ warned, as if Mr. Corbett hadn't said a word.

"I said that's enough, AJ." Mr. Corbett now stood between the boys as they glared at each other. Their teacher looked very serious — and more than a little worried. "I said, get on the bus. *Now*." Mr. Corbett was not the only staff member who had recognized what was going on. Ms. Shorthouse hurried out, along with Mr. Hamilton the counsellor and Ms. Menard the PE teacher.

As more school staff neared, Jackson and the other students reluctantly boarded the bus, but not before he shot a cold look at AJ.

"Now, you go home, too, AJ," Mr. Corbett said. "Before you do or say something you'll regret."

"Who do these people think they are?" Steve said as the Big River bus drove away. "They make some crap up and expect everyone to just do what they want? The Pearsons and the Sullivans built this town." Steve turned to AJ. "We got you," he said. "Harold's statue isn't going anywhere."

"You bet it's not," said AJ. He stormed off to his truck, slammed the door shut, and peeled out of the parking lot, driving a little faster than he should. He could feel the rage coursing through his body as he drove.

Five minutes away from the school, AJ realized he hadn't connected his Bluetooth. CBC Radio was playing on his truck speakers. AJ hardly ever listened to it. The station played music old people liked and did boring things like farm reports. He was about to connect his phone and listen to music to help calm himself down, but when the 3:30 p.m.

news started, he listened, surprised to hear that the damage to the statue led the headlines. The story was no longer local.

"Big River RCMP are investigating an act of vandalism to the Harold Sullivan statue at the high school named after the well-known local pioneer," the news reader said. *"The statue was symbolically covered with orange paint not twenty-four hours after Big River First Nation Chief Robert Thomas demanded that the school district remove the statue and rename the school."*

"Covered? It was trashed," AJ said out loud, furious at how the damage was described.

"When reached for comment, Chief Thomas said that while he does not condone criminal behaviour, he can certainly understand why somebody would undertake such an act."

"Or do it himself," AJ said as he turned onto the long driveway to the Home Ranch. AJ thought back to the messages and posts. He pictured the look on Jackson's face when he saw the damage to the statue and heard the word *racist* echo through his head. That morning AJ had been willing to believe his friend had nothing to do with this. Now? With each passing minute since the confrontation by the bus, he didn't know what to think.

"'Harold Sullivan was a key figure in the institutional racism our people faced in this community for years,' said the chief," the news reader continued. *"'And in the name of truth and reconciliation, this town needs to understand that it is simply not acceptable to have such a person immortalized or to have a scholarship or a school named after him. The people of Big River First Nation and Indigenous people across the country have endured such actions in the past, but we are unwilling to do so moving forward.' And in related breaking news,"* the anchor added, just as AJ reached the house,

"*CBC can confirm that the Big River School District has agreed to hear from Chief Thomas at next Monday's school board meeting, as well as from those who hold different views on the subject. And based on the important place Harold Sullivan holds in the town's history, there are certainly going to be those who disagree. School board meetings are usually boring affairs but this one promises fireworks and the CBC will be there.*"

"Yes, it does," AJ said as he turned off the truck. His dad was right. There was going to be a fight, and the main event would be next Monday night at the school board meeting.

WEDNESDAY MORNING

Another large crowd had gathered when AJ arrived at school. This one included two police vehicles, and if AJ was angry about what had happened yesterday, he was furious today. There was a small dent in Harold's wooden face, as if the statue had been hit with a large hammer. But that wasn't the worst of it. Somebody had painted over the school's name on the large wooden sign that sat beside the entrance, replacing "Harold Sullivan" with the word "racist" in large black letters.

"Can you believe this shit?" Steve slammed the door of his silver Chevy pickup as AJ exited his own truck. "Shorthouse should have known there'd be more damage. She should've put in cameras or security guards."

Before AJ could reply, the bus from Big River First Nation pulled into the turnaround. The First Nations students immediately saw what had happened. Some looked uncomfortably at the damage, while others laughed and broke out their phones to take pictures. Then Jackson stepped off the bus.

"You did this, didn't you?" AJ demanded. "You called my great-grandfather the exact same word that was on the sign yesterday!"

"I did not!" Jackson replied defiantly.

"Like hell you didn't," Steve shouted "You still want to go talk, Jackson?"

"Shorthouse is coming," somebody said, and as the principal arrived, the boys reluctantly separated and walked into school.

The first two classes of the day went very slowly for AJ. He was in Math class with Steve, and the two of them could hardly pay attention to the lesson. "Do you really think Jackson did this?" whispered AJ while their teacher talked about angles and triangles.

"Who else?" Steve sounded certain. "My dad said he was surprised it took this long for it to happen. Bad stuff happened in the past, I'm not denying that, but all Native people want to do now is make us feel bad about it."

"I don't know," AJ said.

"Listen," Steve told him. "It's happening all over the place, and people are too scared to call them out on it. You know that job my dad bid on up in Swan Valley?"

AJ did. Swan Valley was a town about 100 kilometres north of Big River. A copper mine was going in, and the company had put out a contract to log three hundred hectares of land to clear the site. The job was worth millions.

"I know for a fact that my dad's company was supposed to get the contract, but the government made the mining company give it to a Native contractor just because they were Native. It's wrong, AJ. What's going on is wrong, and somebody's got to stand up and say enough is enough. How long do they expect people to pay for mistakes made in the past?"

The bell rang for lunch. AJ and Steve left the school and were planning to go downtown for French fries. It was then they saw Jackson outside, not far from the statue, talking to some of his friends from the First Nation.

"What's next, Jackson?" said Steve. "You gonna burn down the school?"

"Like your great-grandfather helped burn down the Freedom Camp, Steve?" Jackson shot back.

"Come on, you guys, that's enough." AJ was angry about the statue and the things being said about Harold, but the three of them had been playing ball together just a couple of days ago. He could hardly believe how fast things had escalated.

"No, it's not enough," said Steve. "These people need to learn to keep their mouths shut."

"These people?" Jackson took the comment for the insult it was. "I didn't damage that stupid statue, but I'm glad someone did. It should have been done years ago. You and your families are living on stolen land, and that fancy scholarship is paid for out of a racist's blood money."

Things happened quickly. Before AJ knew it, a tidal wave of hot anger raced through him. He rushed toward Jackson and swung his arms, one after the other. He felt his right fist connect with something hard.

"Kick his ass, AJ!" Steve shouted. Then a sharp pain exploded in the side of his head as Jackson swung back, both boys now throwing wild haymakers at each other. AJ felt his own fist land again somewhere on Jackson's head, saw Jackson stagger a little, but then Jackson swung back, his punch landing right on AJ's nose. Stars exploded in front of his eyes and a warm surge of blood poured out onto his shirt.

A strong set of arms wrapped around AJ, pinning his hands, holding him hard, pulling him away.

"Stop it!" AJ recognized the voice as Mr. Corbett's, though it sounded as if it was a thousand kilometres away.

Through his half-closed, teary eyes AJ saw somebody — a teacher or a student, he couldn't tell — do the same thing to Jackson. "I told you to stop this before you did something you regret," said Mr. Corbett, holding AJ tight. "I wish you'd listened to me."

An hour later AJ was still in the school's office, an ice pack on his face, his shirt crusted with dried blood, and his head and hands aching. He sat in a chair across from Ms. Shorthouse's empty desk, feeling sore, sorry for himself, but still angry. AJ was not a fighter, not really. He'd been in a couple of scraps playing hockey but that was different. He'd never had something like this happen to him at school before. He'd never even been in trouble at school either, not for anything serious. This was all a brand-new experience, and he didn't like it at all.

The door opened and Ms. Shorthouse walked back into her office. "I finally managed to get through to your dad," she said, sitting down in her chair. "I told him what happened and that, unfortunately, you're going to be suspended for the rest of the week."

"Please, Ms. Shorthouse, I know what I did was wrong, but I didn't start it. Jackson did."

The principal shook her head. "AJ, fighting at school is a very clear violation of the code of conduct and you know that. Besides, Jackson may very well have insulted Harold Sullivan, but I've talked to a great number of students who witnessed the fight, and they all agree that it was you who started punching."

"So, Jackson gets to talk trash about my family, and you don't do anything about it?" AJ said bitterly.

"Jackson is going home as well, and for the same length of time as you," said Ms. Shorthouse. "And you're both going to refrain from talking to each other or escalating this situation with your friends; whether in person, on social media, or group chats. Things need to calm down around here."

"If it wasn't for Jackson wrecking the statue none of this would have happened!"

"I understand this has been a very emotional time for you," said Ms. Shorthouse calmly. "And I promise you that the school and the RCMP take the vandalism to Harold's statue and the school sign very seriously. There is an active investigation, and I have every faith we will find out who did the damage, but what happened to the sign and the statue does not give you the right to fight a fellow student."

"This is bullshit," said AJ. It was rude and he knew it, but he was too upset to care.

"Listen, AJ," Ms. Shorthouse said. "I grew up here and graduated from this school, too. Your dad, Buck Pearson, and Robert Thomas were a couple of years behind me at school, and I've known your families for more than forty years. I understand what this situation means to both sides, and I know how short tempers are right now, but I will not have you, or Jackson Thomas, or Steve Pearson, or anyone else for that matter, making things worse. And I certainly will not tolerate any more disrespect. Do I make myself clear?"

"Yes, Ms. Shorthouse. I'm sorry." AJ *was* sorry. He liked the principal and under normal circumstances would never have talked to her like that.

"Good," she replied. "Then we can leave this conversation between us and not involve your parents in it. I think you've given them enough to deal with for one day, don't you?"

"Probably," AJ replied sheepishly. "What did my dad say when you called him?" AJ was glad his mom was at a ranch some fifty kilometres from town looking to buy a gelding and that she was way out of cell range. She handled most things better than his dad, but not fights. She was going to go crazy about this.

"You can ask him yourself," said Ms. Shorthouse, handing AJ his phone back. She had taken it from him when he'd been brought to the office. "He's waiting for your call."

"Great," AJ muttered as he tapped on the screen. His dad was going to kill him.

"Hi, Dad," AJ said when the call connected. "Guess Ms. Shorthouse told you, eh?"

"Are you okay?" his dad asked. "I heard you got punched pretty good."

"I'm fine," AJ said. "Bloody nose, a couple of bruises. I've been hurt worse falling off one of Mom's horses."

"What happened?" his dad asked. "And don't leave any-thing out." AJ told him everything, from the confrontation he'd had with Jackson the day before to the moment he'd been dragged into the office.

"You got suspended until Monday. Robert's boy, too?"

"Yeah," AJ said. He was surprised how well his dad seemed to be taking the news. "Mom won't be happy though, will she?"

"Probably not, but I'll talk to her when she gets home. You'll be busy."

"Busy? Doing what?" asked AJ.

"Working. Go home, clean up, and head over to your grandma's place. She's got some chores needing to be done. I've already spoken to her and she's expecting you. I'm not going to have you sleeping in or sitting around on your phone for the rest of the week. Make sure you bring your work clothes."

AJ hung up. "Do I go home now?" he asked Ms. Short-house.

"You do," she said. "And AJ," she added, "Things are go-ing to be very tense around here while this situation with the name and the statue works itself out. While you are on your suspension, don't contact Jackson Thomas, do not come to the school for any reason, and please, whatever you do, don't make things worse."

WEDNESDAY AFTERNOON

"So how was school today?" asked AJ's grandmother, Dorothy Sullivan, when he arrived at her house.

"Ha ha. Very funny," AJ replied. "You know what happened. Dad told you."

"He did," she said. "And you look a sight. That shiner is going to last a few days, and I'm surprised your nose isn't broken. Do you need ice or an Aspirin or something for the pain?"

"I'll be fine. It looks worse than it feels." Truthfully though, AJ's head hurt. He hadn't been punched before, not in a real fight.

"How did your parents take the news?"

"Mom doesn't know yet. She won't be very happy, but Dad wasn't as mad as I'd have thought."

"That doesn't surprise me," said his grandma. "This whole thing with the school name and the statue is hitting your dad pretty hard. Buck Pearson, too, I imagine. Reputation is very important to your dad and he's going to see this as you sticking up for the Sullivans. Besides," she added, "it's not as if your dad can be too hard on you for fighting. He wasn't an angel when he was in school. If I had a dollar for every time Mr. Wiens, the principal back in his day, called me about something your father did . . . "

"Really? Like what?" The conversation was taking an interesting turn and AJ wanted to know more. His father rarely talked about his own time back at Sullivan High School.

"Another day, perhaps," said his grandma. "You have a fence that needs mending, a chicken coop to dung out, and a garden that needs to be dug up. What do you want to do first? There's enough work to keep you going all week."

"The chicken coop, I guess," AJ said. It was the least pleasant of the jobs his grandmother had lined up for him. His father had taught him years ago to get the harder tasks taken care of first. "You want me to put the manure in the compost?"

"Please," she said. "And turn the compost pile over as well. I'll be planting my garden in a month, and I'll need the fertilizer. "Before you go have a quick bite to eat. I made you a ham sandwich. Figured you haven't had a chance to eat lunch yet."

Dorothy Sullivan lived a kilometre down the road from the Home Ranch on a small acreage that had been called The Cottage for as long as people in Big River could remember. It was one of many properties in town the Sullivans owned. For years she and AJ's grandfather, Harold Sullivan Jr., had lived on the ranch, but when AJ's parents got married and had him, they decided to move to the smaller property, just as Harold Sr. had done when AJ's grandparents got married and had his dad. Great-grandmother Bette died not long after Harold Sr. returned home after the Second World War. He never remarried.

When AJ's grandfather died several years back, Grandma Dorothy was invited to move back into the ranch with them, but she liked her independence and stayed put. Besides, she loved The Cottage. It was an older, three-bedroom bungalow, with clapboard siding painted a crisp white. The property was surrounded by a whitewashed wooden fence, and the outbuildings were also painted white.

AJ finished his sandwich and put on his coveralls and pair of rubber boots. He didn't see helping his grandmother as a punishment. He'd been planning on dunging out the chicken coop anyway, even before the fight with Jackson. It was something he did for his grandmother at least three times a year, and it hadn't been done for a couple of months. He put a pitchfork and a shovel in a wheelbarrow and opened the gate to the coop, ignoring the chickens clucking and squawking. The birds could protest all they wanted but they knew the routine the same as AJ did.

Chicken manure was not the nicest smelling thing on his grandmother's farm, but AJ was used to it. He quickly got to work, pitching manure and old straw into the wheelbarrow until it was full. Then he wheeled the heavy barrow out of the coop and across the yard to the compost heap. He emptied the barrow, mixed the fresh manure into the old compost, and returned for a second load. It was amazing, AJ thought, that something as stinky as chicken manure, when composted and added to the soil, could make vegetables grow big and tasty.

Ninety minutes later AJ was done. He'd removed five loads of manure from the coop, put in new straw, fed the chickens, and collected the half-dozen eggs the birds had laid. He was hungry and was looking forward to dinner. His grandma always made great meals and he quickly climbed out of his coveralls and boots, washed off the sweat and the smell at the outside sink, then walked into the house.

"Done the coop," AJ told his grandmother. "And the compost is turned as well. You've got enough to fertilize a quarter section."

"The half-acre I have is enough at my age," she said. "Thank you very much. Dinner is on the table. I figured you'd be hungry."

As always, she outdid herself, and AJ's mouth watered when he saw the jug of ice-cold lemonade, the homemade fried chicken, and potato salad waiting for him. "Peach pie's warming up in the oven," AJ's grandma said as he sat down and tucked into a delicious drumstick. "You might want to save some room for it."

"No worries about that!" said AJ as he heaped potato salad onto his plate. "I can always make room for your pie, Grandma!"

The two made small talk as they ate, AJ's grandmother sipping on a cup of tea and nibbling on a piece of chicken as AJ wolfed down his food. Warm peach pie straight out of the oven covered in vanilla ice cream appeared on the table not long after, and just as he'd promised AJ found room for it.

"I am so stuffed," AJ said as he helped with the dishes.

"It never ceases to amaze me how much a teenage boy can eat," his grandma said as she poured herself and AJ tea. "Your father was the same. It was a good thing we lived on a farm. How was the coop?"

"A cleaning was overdue," AJ admitted. "It was kind of stinky."

"Did you know that your great-grandfather built that coop himself?"

AJ did not. "Really? It must be sixty years old then."

"More like seventy," his grandma said. "The wood's a bit faded, but it's solid. Harold knew how to build, and that coop is going to outlast all of us."

"Great-Grandpa Harold was quite the guy, wasn't he?"

"He was something," she replied. "It may come as a surprise to you, but he loved looking after those birds. In his last few years, he spent hours in that coop, fussing over his hens. The chickens liked him, too, from what I remember. They seemed very happy when Harold was with them."

That was surprising to AJ. Harold Sullivan was a big deal. "Who would have thought Harold would like to hang out with chickens? I mean, he did so much. He built the mill, and he fought in two wars."

"Harold almost never talked about the war — either one," his grandma said, "but I know he saw some horrible things, and he told me that looking after the chickens made him feel better. In those last years, I think the things he'd seen and done had come back to haunt him. He could put on a show in public, but the real Harold was quite different in private."

"I would never have thought that," said AJ.

"There are a lot of other things about Harold people don't know," she told him. "Your grandfather wasn't Harold and Bette's only child, for instance."

"What?" As far as AJ knew, Harold Junior was Harold and Great-Grandma Bette's only child, just like his dad was an only child, and just as AJ was himself.

"They had a little girl named Mary," his grandma explained. "She was born in 1915, not long after Harold left for Europe."

"No way," AJ replied. "What happened to her?"

"She died of a fever after only a couple of months. That sort of thing happened in those days. Harold never met her, only ever saw her in a photo," she said. "Harold wouldn't talk about it. I learned that story from Bette after I married your grandfather."

"Really?"

"Really. Like I said, there are a lot of things about Harold people don't know. Now come and sit, AJ. We can finish cleaning up later. I want to have a serious talk about what happened at school."

AJ told her everything. His grandma sat and listened, not interrupting as AJ spoke. "And when he said we were living on stolen land, I guess I just lost it," AJ said. "And that's when I started punching. Why would he say that, Grandma? The Home Ranch has been in the family for more than a century. We learned about how some land was taken from reserves in Social Studies class, but what does that have to do with us?"

"Get me my iPad, would you? It's on the coffee table in the front room."

"You have an iPad?" AJ was very surprised to hear that piece of information.

"Of course I have an iPad. How else am I supposed to check Facebook and play my games? Are you suggesting someone my age doesn't know how to use technology?"

"No! Yes? I don't know," AJ stuttered. "I guess I'm just a little shocked, is all."

"And I know how to use it for more than just cat videos and crosswords," she added when AJ came back with the item. "Google the *Soldier Settlement Act*."

AJ did as she asked, opened a link, and read quietly.

"What did you learn?" his grandma asked.

"That after the First World War, the government made land available in the west for returning soldiers," said AJ. "It was to let them settle the land, farm, and make a living."

"All soldiers?" she asked.

"No. First Nation soldiers didn't get any." AJ had been a little stunned when he read that.

"And where did much of this land come from?" his grandma asked. "If you haven't found out yet, keep reading."

AJ did, lifting his eyes up from the screen a moment later. "They took a lot of it from the reserves. I knew that."

She nodded. "More than 70,000 acres. The government called it 'surplus land' and removed it from the reserves. White soldiers returning from the war were eligible for the land grants. Soldiers like Harold."

"But what has that got to do with . . . " Then AJ knew. "The Home Ranch. That was part of the grant, wasn't it?" His heart sank. He had no idea the Home Ranch, his family's home for a century, was cut out of the First Nation land.

"The Cottage as well, and a good chunk of land that is now part of town. The land was cut off from the Big River First Nation Reservation, and Harold paid pennies per acre for it. He wasn't the only veteran to get land. Most of the farms and ranches north of town are built on land taken from Big River First Nation."

"Nobody ever told me that," said AJ.

"Like I said. There are things people don't know about Harold — and things they don't know about their own town," said his grandma. "It happened more than a century ago, and even for those who do remember what happened it's 'ancient history,' like your dad called it."

You and your families are living on stolen land, Jackson had said. "I don't think it's ancient history to Jackson's family," said AJ.

"It isn't," she replied. "And when your dad decided to name his scholarship after Harold Sullivan, I think he woke up a few ghosts — and they're not about to go back to sleep anytime soon."

THURSDAY MORNING

"It took some convincing, but the school district put security guards at the high school last night," AJ's dad said that morning at breakfast. "If they'd done that after the first incident, there wouldn't have been any more."

"And maybe a certain someone wouldn't have got into a fight and been suspended," AJ's mom said.

"Maybe," AJ said as he ate his eggs. His father had been philosophical about the suspension, but his mom had torn a strip off him when she got back home, just as he'd predicted.

"But there wasn't any more damage?" his mom asked.

"No," his dad said. "I had one of my foremen drive past the school first thing this morning. The only thing there were the guards and the news truck."

"That's good. More vandalism is the last thing we need. Things are bad enough with that TV crew up from the city."

As if things couldn't get any worse, a couple of reporters with their satellite truck and cameras had made the trip up to Big River to cover the school board meeting and get background information on Harold Sullivan, no doubt.

"They need to go back to where they're from and mind their own business," his dad said. "The superintendent, Julie Sandusky, and the rest of the school board better show some backbone at the meeting on Monday. The school's name and the statue are left alone if they want one single dollar of that scholarship. It will come with Harold's name attached or not at all. He built this town, and the school district should be proud of students who demonstrate grit like he did."

"When Harold got the land for the Home Ranch, it came from the federal government, right?" AJ had been wanting to ask his father the question since yesterday afternoon but had only worked up the nerve now.

"It did," said his dad. "Lots of soldiers got land as a thank-you for their service, and to help build up the west. Harold got a half section of wilderness and turned it into a home."

"But it wasn't really wilderness, though," AJ said cautiously. "I was talking to Grandma yesterday, and she said that the land used to belong to Big River First Nation and the government gave it away."

"Did she?" His father took a long sip of his coffee before he continued. "It was a long time ago, and the land was wilderness, son. It was part of the reserve, but it wasn't being used. It was just trees and besides, the First Nation still has hundreds of acres that they log and ranch, and they can take as many fish from the river as they want."

"I didn't know that," said AJ's mom. "I thought it was Crown land."

"Like I said, it happened a long time ago and the world has moved on." His dad sounded a little defensive. "Now you need to finish your breakfast and move on as well, right to your grandmother's house. You've got a lot more work to do today."

Even though he knew his father didn't want to talk about this, AJ pressed. "But Dad, knowing that the Home Ranch and other properties in town used to be part of the reserve kind of explains a little about what Robert said, doesn't it?"

"I said, the world has moved on. This is ancient history," his dad snapped, using the same term he'd used the day before. His father didn't just sound defensive anymore. He was getting riled up.

"But it would kind of justify part of what Jackson's dad is talking about, wouldn't it? I mean if somebody took a chunk of land from the Home Ranch and gave it away, we sure would be upset, and it's not like we would ever forget about it."

"AJ," growled his dad. "I said drop it. Finish your breakfast and get going to your grandmother's. I don't want to hear another word about this."

"Yes, sir." His father didn't use that tone often, but AJ knew enough not to push his luck when he did.

"Good. And, AJ," his dad continued, "if you happen to see any of those reporters from down south?"

"Yes, Dad?" AJ replied.

"Don't talk to them. And if they come snooping around your grandmother's house, do your best to make sure she doesn't talk to them either. She's my mother and I love her, but sometimes she says things she shouldn't."

★ ★ ★

Today was fence repair day. At least day one of the job for AJ. His grandma's tidy little property was surrounded by a fence made from rails and horizontal two-by-fours placed between them. Like the rest of her place, the rails and boards were painted white, but it had been a couple of years since the fence had been tended to, and repairs were needed.

It had been a heavy snow year and the ploughs had pushed great piles off the roads into the ditches. Some of these piles had broken the boards. Another section of fence had been scorched in a spring grass fire and more boards were old and rotting. AJ's job was simple: pull all the old and broken boards off the rails, take them to the dump, get fresh lumber, and fix the fence.

AJ figured that the job would take at least two days. He got to work with a hammer and crowbar. It wasn't hard work, but it was time-consuming as AJ worked methodically along the fence line, fixing fifty-metres of fence at a time, tearing off the damaged boards, and driving his truck along the line so he could toss the broken wood into the box.

He liked country music and listened to Morgan Wallen and Luke Bryan as he worked, grateful that the day was sunny and the bugs hadn't come out yet. Maybe the only thing AJ didn't like about Big River was the mosquitoes and the blackflies. They could be awful, especially after a wet spring when large pools of water lay in the ditches.

Three hours after starting the job, the truck was full of old two-by-fours. AJ had worked faster than he'd first thought and there were fewer boards to repair than anticipated. Next step was to drop the wood at the dump and then head to the mill to get new boards.

AJ had been to the mill a million times. He knew every square centimetre of the place, from the lunchroom to the office where his dad and the other managers worked, to the sorting yard where the logs were piled, the mill where they were cut to size, the kiln where the boards were dried, and the planer where each board was smoothed before sales.

AJ loved the mill. He loved the smell of cut wood and bark, the sound of the saws, the clank of the conveyer chains, the rumble of heavy equipment that loaded logs and pallets of wood, and he was grateful beyond words he was part of it. His dad had made sure that AJ got the opportunity to work in every area of the mill, and AJ had spent time doing everything from cleaning up to running saws to sorting the lumber to working in the office where he was learning the business side of the operation.

In the ten years since AJ's father had taken over the business from his own father, the mill had modernized. Lasers guided the saws now, to make sure not a single scrap of wood was wasted. Instead of burning the hog fuel — the leftover sawdust and bark like they used to — Sullivan Sawmills now shipped it south to a biofuel plant outside of the city, where it was turned into clean power for hundreds of homes.

Sullivan Sawmills provided good, well-paying jobs for more than a hundred people in Big River and Big River First Nation, and as he walked into the sales office the anger he felt at Jackson and Robert Thomas returned. His dad was right. Maybe a hundred years ago the Big River First Nation lost a bit of land they weren't using, and maybe it wasn't fair that First Nation veterans didn't get treated the same way, but when AJ thought about the good the sawmill was doing for both town and First Nation, AJ could not believe that anyone would be so ungrateful for things that happened a century ago.

"Your dad said you'd probably be stopping by." Mr. Knizek, the sales manager for Sullivan Sawmills looked up from his desk when AJ entered the office. "I see you took a couple of lumps, Alex Junior. I hope you put him in his place. You don't mess with the Sullivans in this town."

"I guess so." AJ wasn't surprised that Mr. Knizek had heard about the fight. No doubt the entire town had by now.

"Instead of school, you are fixing your grandmother's fence, eh? Good use of your time. You know what they say about idle hands. How much wood you need?" AJ loved how Mr. Knizek talked. He'd come to Canada from Prague in the 1980s, a young man seeking a better life. He'd found it here. Mr. Knizek hardly had a penny to his name when he ended up in Big River. Harold Junior had hired him, and his grandparents had treated Mr. Knizek like he was a son, even letting him stay at their home until he was settled. Mr. Knizek was one in a long line of people whose lives had been made better by the mill Harold had built — and one of many who owed the Sullivans a great deal.

"Better give me four dozen studs, please," said AJ. A stud was an eight-foot long two-by-four and AJ ordered extra in case he discovered more boards to replace. Mr. Knizek wrote out a sales slip and gave it to AJ. The Sullivans could have gotten their wood for free but that was not how they did business.

"Done. Tell Dorothy I put it on her account and give her my love. Your grandmother is a fine lady. Head out to the yard and help yourself."

"Is Dad around?" AJ asked.

"Yes, but on an important call right now and can't be disturbed, but I'll tell him you came by. And, Alex Junior," said Mr. Knizek. "Good for you for sticking up for the family. That Robert Thomas needs to know his place as well. Your family has been very good to him. You don't bite the hand that feeds."

AJ loaded up the wood and with his truck sagging on its springs under the heavy load of lumber, he headed back to his grandmother's. His grandma came out to meet him when he arrived.

"Lunch is ready," she said. "Unload your truck, wash up, and come in for a bite. If I know you, you're probably famished."

AJ piled the lumber outside of his grandma's small barn, washed up, and went inside to eat. Today's lunch was ham and cheese sandwiches on his grandma's still-warm home-made bread and just like yesterday, AJ felt as if he'd burst when he finished his meal.

"So last night I asked Dad if he knew about where the land for the Home Ranch came from," said AJ.

"How did he take that question?"

"Not great. Ancient history. All in the past."

"Did he say anything else?" asked his grandma, her voice sounding very much as if she already knew the answer.

"I don't think he was stoked that you told me." AJ left out the part about what his dad said about talking to the reporters. He knew his grandmother. She might be small and old, but she was as tough as nails and she would do what she wanted to do, regardless of what her son thought.

"That isn't surprising," she said. "Your dad is a chip off the old Sullivan block."

"I should get back to work," said AJ. "I've got a lot of boards to nail up."

"You can do that tomorrow," his grandma said. "Nails and tools are in the barn, but I have a different job for you right now."

"Like what?" AJ wasn't expecting that.

"I need you to go to the library and get me a book. And while you're there, I want you to do a little research."

"Research? What kind of research?" AJ's grandmother was making no sense.

"Research about Harold," she said.

"Why would I do that, Grandma? I think I know who my great-grandfather was, don't you?"

"You may know family history, AJ," she said, "and you may know the legend of Harold Sullivan, but he was my father-in-law, and I knew him personally. There's a lot of things about Harold that people remember, but there is also a great deal that's either forgotten — or ignored. The TV people and Big River First Nation are going to be doing their homework on Harold Sullivan and they will dig things up. You need to know what he was like as well."

"I don't think Dad would be happy with either of us if I did this." AJ loved his grandmother, but he was reluctant to cross his father, especially after his reaction that morning.

"What is the family motto, AJ? I know you have it memorized. What comes after Hard Work?"

"Integrity. Why?"

"What does that word mean to you?"

"I didn't know you were an English teacher, Grandma," AJ joked. "I guess it means being honest and doing the right thing."

"Those are good definitions," she replied. "And right now, doing the right thing is going to the library and getting me my book."

"A book made out of paper, Grandma?" he teased. "Why don't you read it on your iPad?"

"I have plenty of those in my Kindle," she said. "But every now and then I like the feeling of a book in my hand. Besides, you'll be spending some time going through the archives of the Big River *Gazette*. Every copy since the first day they began publishing is stored on microfilm, and I want you to see what that paper said about your great-grandfather over the years."

"What's microfilm?" AJ had never heard that word before.

His grandma rolled her eyes. "And you think I'm the one who doesn't know technology? When you get to the library see Ms. Wallace. Tell her what you're looking for and she'll set you up, but before you go, I'm going to give you a couple rolls of quarters."

"Quarters? Like the coins?" AJ was more confused than ever. He couldn't remember the last time he used anything but his bank card or his phone to pay for things.

"I'm going to give you quite a few, and you'll need them all. The stories of Big River and Harold Sullivan are very much intertwined. Start with July 1914," said his grandma. "When the world, Canada, and Harold Sullivan, went to war."

THURSDAY AFTERNOON

"Alex Sullivan Junior, what a surprise! I can't remember the last time I saw you here!" Ms. Wallace said as AJ walked into the library.

"You have a book for my grandmother?" AJ asked.

Ms. Wallace did. She reached up onto the shelf behind her and gave AJ a thick paperback. "That Dorothy sure does like her horror books."

"She does?" AJ looked at the title and was surprised. This was not the sort of book he'd have pictured his grandmother reading.

"She does, and you might want to try one out as well. Shouldn't you be at school, by the way?"

AJ wasn't sure how to respond. "I'm taking the day off," he finally said.

"That's right; you got into a scrap with that Thomas boy

the other day. I did hear something about that." The fight with Jackson was no secret, and people in Big River, in all small towns for that matter, gossiped. As the town librarian there was no doubt Ms. Wallace would hear all of it.

"Anything else I can do for you since you're here? Historical research? Genealogy, maybe?" she said knowingly.

"Grandma called, didn't she?" AJ said. "To make sure I did what she wants."

"She did. Come into the back room. I've got the microfilm reader all set up and I've pulled the copies of the Gazette already. Did your grandmother tell you how to make copies?"

AJ felt the rolls of coins in his pocket. "She gave me a bunch of quarters. You haven't upgraded to tap yet, I guess."

"You are a funny young man, AJ Sullivan. I've loaded the copier with paper just for you. Dorothy said you would be making a lot of copies."

Ms. Wallace led AJ into the archive room. It was a small place, not much bigger than an office, full of filing cabinets and a couple of machines. "Watch carefully while I set up the reader. It's low-tech compared to what you kids are used to, and it's a little finicky. You don't want to mess up a roll of microfilm. Now what year do you want to start?"

"1914, I guess." That was the year his grandmother had suggested, the start of the First World War.

"1914 it is, then." Ms. Wallace loaded up the first roll. "July 29th, 1914. The *Gazette* ran a special edition. War was declared on the 28th but it took a day for the news to reach Big River. Put the quarters in the machine and hit print for every copy you want."

"Canada Declares War!" The headline was in big black letters followed by the latest news from France and London. AJ read the story and then looked at the advertisements in the paper. Clothes, farming equipment, and food. The same things people in Big River used today, but the ads looked different, more *old-timey*, than the ones the *Gazette* had now.

After the special war edition, the paper reverted to its usual printing, once a week on Mondays. Even after all these years, the paper still came out on that day. Each edition was short, and it didn't take AJ long to scan the stories looking for any mention of Harold. It wasn't until he reached the end of September that he found his great-grandfather.

"Lieutenant Sullivan and the rest of the Big River Lads in the Princess Patricia's prepare to fight for King and Country." There was even a picture. He had seen it before, in an album his dad kept on the bookshelf. AJ recognized Harold's face in a crowd of uniformed men, guns slung on their backs, smiles on their faces. AJ knew Harold had been an officer. He had served in the local volunteer militia before the war started, one of the few men in the country with any sort of military experience at all, and he was quickly commissioned into the regular army.

AJ read the story, read how Harold and the others were in Quebec, at Valcartier and were preparing to ship off for England. He looked at their faces again. Such young men. AJ had studied the First World War at school. It was a bloodbath and the young men from Big River, some his own age had no idea what they were marching into. Thirty men from Big River fought in the war. Fewer than twenty came home.

There was no other mention of Harold until June of 1917. *"Big River Local a Hero of Vimy."* Harold Sullivan, a captain now, was part of the Canadian corps who had stormed Vimy Ridge in April and won a tremendous victory for the Allies.

"Captain Sullivan led his men fearlessly through No-Man's-Land. They reached the German lines where they engaged in ferocious hand-to hand-combat. Though wounded, Captain Sullivan kept up the fight, knocking out three German machine gun nests and securing the line. At a ceremony at Buckingham Palace, Captain Sullivan was awarded the Military Cross by King George V himself."

AJ knew that Harold had been given a medal by the king. The entire town did, and it was a key part of the Harold Sullivan Legend. In the paper there was another familiar photograph of his great-grandfather, in uniform with his medal pinned to his chest, standing at attention. Although Harold looked proud, he also seemed tired, and looked much older than the man who had left Big River. AJ felt a swell of pride. He couldn't imagine fighting in a war like that. Harold was a hero. How dare Jackson and his family say such terrible things.

The next mention of Harold was from the spring of 1919 when he and the other Big River boys came home. AJ read how the government, grateful for the service of men like Harold, gave them land at a terrific discount. There was no mention in the paper where that land came from. AJ moved on, month after month, year and after year. He read about the opening of the Sullivan Sawmill and there were several other articles about Harold, but the other stories about life in Big River one hundred years ago were equally fascinating to him. It wasn't until AJ had reached the 1930s that he realized there had hardly been any mention of the Big River First Nation. It was as if that twin community did not exist.

In 1939, and for the second time in twenty-five years, AJ read that men from Big River heeded the call when war was declared. Harold, now in his mid-fifties, volunteered to serve his country once more. AJ knew Harold had gone back into the army, but he didn't know that this time Harold, commissioned as a major, served in the Canadian Corps headquarters just outside of London, England.

AJ read about the war, though there was little mention of Harold again until 1946 when he returned home with the rest of the Big River soldiers. A parade was held in their honour. AJ saw a photo he'd never seen before: Harold, sitting in the back of a convertible car in his dress uniform, waving to the crowd. Harold was sixty now, but his eyes looked older than that. AJ wondered just what those eyes had seen in the nearly ten years Harold had served his country in the two bloodiest wars the world had ever known.

Not long after the parade, Harold's name appeared in almost every weekly paper. He was elected mayor in 1947 and was soon putting his mark on the politics of Big River. Sometimes in ways that made AJ quite uncomfortable.

"'Of course, Indian children from the Big River reserve can't attend the town school,'" said Harold in one interview. "'The *Big River school is paid for by Big River taxpayers, of which Sullivan Sawmills is the largest by far. Indians don't pay taxes so why should they — or anyone else — expect them to benefit? Besides,'"* Harold added, *"'There is a perfectly good residential school for Indian children at Sturgeon Lake. The school was built to help these people assimilate into modern life, and that is where they need to go. It is the* job of the Indian Agent and the RCMP to ensure they attend, and as mayor of Big River I will make certain that happens.'"

"Sullivan was a driving force in sending our children to residential schools." AJ remembered Robert Thomas saying that in a much more recent edition of the Gazette. AJ's growing discomfort exploded when he found the story he had been waiting to read, in a copy of the paper from September 1949.

The headline ran across the front page: *The Clean-up of the 'Freedom' Camp.*

"For the last two years, Mayor Sullivan has spoken of the need to do away with the so-called Freedom Camp, which, in reality, is little more than a squatter's camp made from cull lumber and tarpaper. Today, with Councillor Buck Pearson and a crew from Sullivan Mills at his side, the mayor did just that.

The Indians from Big River Reserve have been squatting illegally on town land since 1947. Despite repeated demands to decamp they stayed, but with fears of more Indians joining the six families already living in the camp, Mayor Sullivan warned the existing squatters the camp would be cleaned out immediately as they were there illegally, their presence blocking the planned expansion of a new subdivision off Prospector Avenue.

It was stated by a bystander that Mayor Sullivan must have no heart at all to burn out these families, but the mayor responded that he had heart enough to let them live on town land for two years and not charge them rent.

As far as the Gazette *is concerned, the people of Big River can thank Harold Sullivan for ridding us of an eyesore and making the town a more beautiful and desirable place to live."*

Along with the story was a photo of Harold Sullivan at the scene, his trademark hatchet in his hand. AJ felt his stomach turn a little as he printed the page, the latest in thirty or so copies he'd made since arriving at the library.

AJ turned off the machine, replaced the roll into its canister, and thanked Ms. Wallace for her time. There were another three rolls of microfilm, rolls that would take AJ up to 1970 when Harold died at eighty-five, but AJ had read enough about his great-grandfather for one day at least. It was time to take Grandma her book and then go home.

"Did you learn anything interesting?" his grandma asked when he reached her house.

"Maybe more than I wanted to," AJ admitted.

"You want to talk about it?" she asked.

AJ did not. "I'm just trying to wrap my mind around what I read. There was some hard stuff to see."

"The truth is like that," his grandma said. "Thanks for the book and I'll see you tomorrow. Finish my fence and your punishment will be complete."

"Spending time with you is hardly punishment." AJ smiled, glad his grandmother didn't press. He really didn't feel like talking about what he'd learned, even to her. AJ gave her a hug and kiss goodbye, hopped back into his truck, and drove toward home. Not thirty seconds after he left her house, his phone rang.

"Enjoying your vacay?" It was Steve Pearson. AJ hadn't talked to any of his friends since his suspension and had done his best to stay off social media. It was nice to hear a friendly voice.

"How's school?" AJ asked.

"No more fights, surprisingly," Steve said. "Things aren't

exactly normal, though. Shorthouse must be walking about twenty kilometres a day patrolling the school, keeping the peace."

"Nothing else?" AJ was glad to hear there hadn't been another scrap.

"That's what I'm calling about." AJ could hear the excitement in Steve's voice. "Me and a couple of the guys are organizing a rally."

"Rally? What are you talking about?"

"It was my dad's idea. There's no way we're going to let Robert Thomas talk the school board into renaming the school and removing Harold's statue without a fight," said Steve. "We're calling it SOSS: save our school and our statue. Pretty cool, eh? Harold and my great-grandfather helped build this town, and we're not going to let anyone destroy his reputation. We're going to wear our school jerseys, too. Everyone will be repping the red and blue."

"Yeah, cool," AJ said, though as far as he was concerned, what he'd learned about his great-grandfather today wasn't exactly the sort of thing a person would want to be remembered for. "When are you holding the rally?"

"This Saturday in front of the school," said Steve. "There's gonna be a lot of people showing up."

"I don't know," AJ said uncertainly. "I'm still on a suspension, and Ms. Shorthouse told me not to do anything to make things worse."

"AJ! Seriously?" Steve sounded as if he couldn't believe what he was hearing. "This is bigger than a stupid suspension or what Jackson's dad thinks. I'm not going to let those people keep saying crap about us!"

Those people. The phrase made AJ uncomfortable. "I know," he conceded.

"Besides," Steve said, "I told everyone you're going to give a speech!"

"You said I would do what?" AJ wasn't certain he heard correctly.

"AJ! You have to speak. Our ancestors built this town into something important when Robert and his ancestors were living in tepees. They didn't build the mill or the rink or the school. We did. Big River would be nothing but a shitty little fishing camp if we hadn't showed up. Nobody on the reserve hunts with bows and arrows. They have rifles and pickups and computers because of Harold and my great-grandfather and the others who civilized this place. It's about time they were reminded of that."

FRiDaY MORNiNG

"I heard some of the students are gathering at the school tomorrow," AJ's dad said at breakfast. "Defending their school, their heritage, and our family name."

"I heard that too." AJ wasn't surprised his dad knew. It was Buck Pearson's idea, after all. Steve and some of the other students had been blasting information out on social media, and both the *Gazette* and the CBC had covered the rally on their websites. AJ's father didn't even use Facebook, but that didn't matter. Word of the rally had spread quickly in Big River.

"Those are the kind of youth this scholarship is meant to support. You're going to be speaking as well, right?"

AJ took some time before responding. Two days ago, he would have been organizing the rally himself, but now? Harold might have been his great-grandfather, but what AJ had learned made him a little uneasy. "I don't think I can, Dad.

Ms. Shorthouse said I couldn't be on school grounds when I was on suspension."

"Your suspension was for three days," his dad said. "Wednesday, Thursday, Friday. Saturday's day number four. Midnight tonight you are free and clear by my reckoning."

"Yeah, I guess, it's just that I was also told not to do anything to make things worse, and I don't know if I should." AJ tried the same argument on his father as he had with Steve. It failed today as well.

AJ's dad put down his coffee cup and looked at his son intently. "Am I actually hearing this?" AJ swallowed. He knew how his father could get worked up, and he was seeing it happen now. "How could things be worse? There are people out there who are trying to insult the memory of your great-grandfather just because he was white. They want to brush him away as if the fact he dedicated his entire life to this town meant nothing, and you are telling me you don't want to make things worse?"

AJ's mom intervened. "Alex, I think what AJ is trying to say is that . . . "

His father slammed a hand down on the table. "I don't care what he is *trying* to say. I care more about what he is *going to do*. I will not let my son stand on the sidelines and do nothing while other people step up for our family!"

"Do nothing?!" AJ was getting worked up now, too. "I got suspended for fighting for this family, in case you don't remember! It was me who got hit and me who got suspended, not you!"

"AJ! Alex!" AJ's mom said sharply. "That's enough, the both of you."

"Dad," AJ said, trying to calm down, "I know what you're saying, but there are things about Grandpa Harold that —"

"The only thing about Harold you need to concern yourself with is that he is your family. Am I clear? You are damn well going to be there front and centre at the rally on Saturday, AJ. The Sullivan family honour is on the line, and you will be there to defend it."

"I'll see you when I get back from Grandma's." AJ stood up and left the table. His breakfast was only half-eaten, but he wasn't hungry anymore. *Stand on the sidelines?* His eye was still black, and his cheek was still swollen. Hardly the sort of thing that happened to a person who stood on the sidelines.

AJ was outraged at his father for questioning his loyalty to the family as he went down the driveway to his grandmother's house, tires spinning on the gravel as he hit the gas. He spent the trip wrestling with his emotions, and it wasn't until he pulled into his grandma's driveway, that he began to understand that while he was angry at his dad, he was also angry at Harold. He remembered the photo . . . saw Harold's smile and his trademark stance, hatchet held proudly.

AJ pictured the houses burning. He was furious that the person he'd idolized his entire life, the person who he had even tried to model his own life after, had done such a horrible thing. He was furious at just how righteous Harold had looked, and that the *Gazette* and the town of Big River itself had cheered his actions. He couldn't believe how blatant the racism was back in those days.

But was it just in those days? On the surface, it had felt to AJ that people got along well enough in Big River these days but Robert's petition seemed to have opened up some old wounds. Tempers were rising, his friends and family were using uncomfortable words, and things were getting out of hand. Up until just the other day AJ would never, not for one minute, have considered that maybe Robert Thomas and the people of the First Nation had legitimate reasons to question Harold Sullivan's legacy. Now, it was all very confusing.

AJ loaded up the two-by-fours into the back of his truck and tried to put the thoughts from his mind. Wood ready to go, AJ went into the barn, the old wooden door creaking as he did. His grandmother had put her small tool chest on the shelf by the door, right next to a large box of nails. AJ took a minute to look around the old barn. It was one of his favourite places on his grandma's property. It smelled of hay and old wood and horses.

AJ was an only child and when he was little, he would come over to his grandma's with his friends, especially Steve. They would pretend the barn was a fort or a castle. They would play hide-and-go-seek in the barn and the other outbuildings, and when AJ was visiting his grandmother by himself, he would feed the animals and help dig potatoes and shell peas while she told stories. He loved the barn. It was a large part of his childhood, as much as the legend of Harold Sullivan. *And why wouldn't it be?* AJ thought as he put the tools and the nails in the truck. Just as Harold had built the chicken coop he had built the barn as well, back before the Second World War, with wood from the Sullivan Sawmill.

AJ would never consider himself a carpenter, but he knew how to hang boards on fenceposts, and by the time the mid-day sun hung high in the blue sky above, he'd finished the job. The boards would need to be whitewashed, but AJ knew his grandmother would do that. She might have been getting older and slowing down a little, but she wasn't about to download to AJ or anybody else a job she could do for herself. He drove back to the house, washed up and went inside.

"Let me guess?" his grandma said when AJ walked in. "You're starving, right?"

AJ laughed. "How did you know?"

"Because you're a teenage boy, and teenage boys are always hungry, especially after putting in four hours of work. I've made roast beef sandwiches and potato salad. Does that work for you?"

It certainly did, and for the third day in a row AJ ate until he thought his stomach would burst. After lunch his grandma poured tea. "Are you going to tell me what's going on, Alex Junior?" she asked. "Something's bothering you. I can see it all over your face."

"Have you heard about the rally that's happening at the school tomorrow?" AJ asked.

"The Save our School and Statue thing? It came up on my Facebook feed."

"Steve Pearson organized it," AJ told her. "There's supposed to be hundreds of students going, pretty much the entire school except for . . . "

"The kids from Big River First Nation," said his grandma.

"I'm supposed to speak at it to defend our family honour, but after learning all that stuff about Harold, especially how he had those homes burned down?" AJ left the rest unsaid.

"What does your father think?" his grandma asked.

"You really need ask to that question, Grandma? You know my dad better than just about anyone."

"Did you tell him about what you read in the *Gazette* archives?"

"I tried, Grandma, I really did, but he wasn't in any mood to listen, and we were both just getting mad at each other, so I left and came here."

"That was probably a good idea," she said. "The Sullivan men do have a bit of a temper, but maybe you inherited some common sense from your mother."

"I don't know what to do," AJ sighed. "If I don't go to the rally, my dad is going to kill me, and I'll probably lose my best friend and pretty much every other friend I have, too. And if I do go? I'm supposed to have integrity, to do the right thing. Dad harps on me about that all the time, but after learning about some of the stuff Harold said and did, I'm not sure I can defend it by saying that's *just how it was back in those days*. And the way Steve and some of the other guys are talking about people from the First Nation? What should I do, Grandma? Can you just tell me?"

"It's not that simple, AJ," she said. "This is a decision that you are going to have to make by yourself. You're going to have to search your heart and do what you think is right."

"But I'm not sure I know what right is, and that's the problem!" AJ said, getting to the core of his dilemma. "Sticking up for your family is right, but knowing that your family has done something that isn't good and speaking up about that is right, too."

"Upstairs in the attic, there's a steamer trunk," his grandma said after a moment. "There may be something inside it that can help you."

"A what?" AJ had never heard of such a thing.

"A steamer trunk. It's like an old-fashioned suitcase that people took on boat and train rides. The one in the attic dates to the First World War. I've never shown it to you. It's been up there for ages. I don't think your dad even knows it exists."

"I'm sure that's interesting, Grandma, but I don't know what that has to do with anything we're talking about," said AJ.

"It may have a lot to do with what we're talking about," his grandma said. "It's Harold's. There are all sorts of items in there: mementos, documents, goodness knows what else. Nobody's opened that trunk since the day Harold Sullivan died. Perhaps you should have a look at what's in there, AJ. You might find something that can help you make your decision — one way or the other."

FRiDay AFTeRNOON

The Cottage's attic was not one of those scary sorts of attics you'd see in horror movies or read about in the books AJ's grandmother enjoyed. There were no creepy mannequins, no creaking floors, no dark and mysterious, spider-web-covered corners. This attic was more like a third floor to the small house, accessed through a door and up a steep flight of stairs at the end of the upstairs hallway.

AJ hadn't been up in the attic for years. There were many other fun places to play on the farm, and he'd almost forgotten about it. The attic was neat and tidy, the roof joists and insulation tucked underneath a wooden shiplap ceiling. The overhead light was covered in a simple shade that cast a warm glow. Rarely used or not, AJ's grandmother was not the sort of person to let a bare bulb hang down from the ceiling.

As AJ walked deeper inside, the attic smelled a little

musty but not wet and mouldy. There was a small window at the far end and he opened it to let in some fresh air. With light and air streaming in, he looked for the steamer trunk and soon found it, next to an old rocking chair in the corner, right where his grandmother told him it would be.

The trunk was old, AJ could tell right away. It was a large, rectangular, metal-covered box with large hinges and a clasp at the front where, at one time, a padlock would have been placed to secure the contents. There were stickers on the lid and sides. Some had faded beyond reading but others were legible with their logos still visible. Canadian Pacific's beaver on a shield. Cunard Line's cutaway ship; shipping and railway line symbols from more than a century ago. Just looking at them made AJ feel as if the attic was a time machine.

AJ opened the lid. He was expecting the hinges to squeak, but instead the trunk opened without a sound, like the hinges had been oiled recently, instead of sitting here undisturbed for half a century.

The first thing AJ saw was an old army jacket, folded carefully, sitting on top of the rest of the contents. He gently lifted it out. It was khaki, with brass buttons and a crown on the shoulder patches. This was from World War Two, AJ knew. The crown was the insignia for Major. It looked as if it would fit him and though AJ was tempted to try it on, he resisted the urge. He knew what his great-grandfather had done to earn that crown and uniform, and it felt disrespectful to wear it.

Beneath that was an older, light-brown one. AJ refolded the major's jacket, set it aside, and removed the other one. *And this is when you were a captain in 1917.*

AJ said to himself. He knew what the three pips on the shoulder patches meant as well. After all, AJ knew all about Harold's life. Or at least he'd thought he did, AJ corrected himself. Over the last three days at his grandmother's house, he'd learned far more than he'd wanted to about his great-grandfather.

Underneath was a bar full of Harold's medals. AJ recognized the Military Cross right away. It was silver, with crowns embossed on each point, and *GR* in the middle where the arms of the cross intersected. There were other medals as well. Campaign medals from two world wars arranged in a line along the bar, each representing battle, a campaign, or an act of individual bravery.

AJ had seen the medals in pictures but never in real life. He thought again about what a courageous man Harold had been, and despite what he'd found out recently he still felt some of the anger toward the Thomas family emerge. Maybe Harold wasn't perfect, but he was a hero and he deserved more respect than what was happening to him now.

AJ carefully put the second uniform aside and for the next hour went through the trunk item by item. There were dozens of photos of Harold, the Sullivan family, and Big River going back from the early sixties to the first years of the twentieth century. It was the most unusual thing for AJ to see them, especially pictures of places he knew, like the Home Ranch. There were small trinkets as well. Some, AJ guessed, were souvenirs Harold had picked up in the two world wars, while others were more local, like a horseshoe that would have meant something special to Harold, but whose significance was long forgotten.

AJ's heart jumped when he saw the hatchet. There it was, underneath a picture of Harold and his great-grandmother's wedding. The very hatchet that no doubt Harold had used in his own life, the one carved from wood in front of AJ's school, the one in all the photos of his late relative — including the one where Harold stood smiling in front of the burning Freedom Camp.

AJ put the hatchet down and kept digging through the trunk. As he neared the bottom there were books. Some were old novels by Dickens and Stevenson, stories and adventure books Harold would have read as a young man. There were also bundles of old papers. AJ thumbed through them. Mostly they were legal and financial documents and they looked dry and boring to AJ. But there was also a series of leather-bound journals.

Harold kept a diary?

And not just one book. There were almost two dozen of them, some as old as 1914 when Harold first went to war. For any local historian, the books would be a treasure. AJ looked through the oldest one first, and read, in Harold's neat cursive, about his great-grandfather's experiences in the war. He read about places he'd studied in school. Vimy, Passchendaele, and other famous battles. And AJ read how Harold was heartbroken when he received the telegram from home that his little daughter, the child he'd never met, had died.

If he had wanted, AJ could have spent a month reading the journals, but there was one time in Harold's life he was most interested in at this moment: *1948–1950.* Harold was a meticulously organized man, and it took AJ no time to find the entries he wanted.

AJ sat in the old rocking chair next to the trunk. After a few seconds of searching, he found September 1949 and began to read. AJ finished the first page and when he turned it over two pieces of paper slipped out of the journal. AJ panicked for a moment, thinking he'd ripped the fragile book but when he picked the pieces up, he saw that the handwriting wasn't Harold's and the pages had been ripped out of a different book.

AJ read them, then read again, and again a third time. At first what he saw confused him, but halfway through the second reading he realized what they were — though he didn't want to believe it.

After he read the pages one last time, AJ put them back into the journal and read the rest of Harold's entry for the day the Freedom Camp was burned. AJ felt ill when he'd finished. He wasn't sure what to think but he knew for certain he had to show the journal and the loose sheets to his grandmother.

He put Harold's things neatly back into the trunk and hurried down the stairs. His grandma looked up from her iPad. "You were up there an awful long time. I was about to come and get you. "What did you find?"

"This," AJ said. "From September of 1949. I don't want to believe it, Grandma. It can't be true, can it?"

"Give me a moment," she said as she put on her glasses. AJ watched anxiously as she read both the entry and the two pages AJ had found tucked into the journal. "That is something," she sighed when she had finished.

"Is this true? Did you know about this?" AJ had been shocked and upset before, but he was now heartbroken that there was even the possibility of what he'd read being true.

"There were a few rumours," his grandma said, "but Harold and the other men there that day insisted they were nothing but lies. And, as you can see, there was no follow-up by the authorities."

"How, Grandma? I mean, how could somebody be responsible for something like that and go on with their life as if nothing happened?"

"If it happened," she said. "I'm not saying it didn't, but we are talking about an event from more than seventy years ago and what you read was never proven."

"Do you really believe that?" AJ asked. "That it was just a rumour?"

His grandma took a breath before responding. "In my heart of hearts, I believe that this terrible thing did happen."

"So why was there no investigation?"

"I suppose it was because there was no proof except for the testimony of one person, and you can see with your own eyes how little that man's word was valued, especially when compared to Harold's. Your great-grandfather was the mayor and a war hero, after all. He held a great deal of power in this community, and I think the police decided to believe Harold — or at the very least they didn't want to not believe him, which isn't quite the same thing. After all, they wouldn't look good themselves, would they?"

"It's not right, Grandma," said AJ. "It's just not right. I know Harold was this legend and that he helped build the town, but if this is true?"

"Big River's a bit of a tinder keg right now, and this could set the whole town on fire if it comes out," said his grandma. "So, what are you going to do about it?"

"I don't know," admitted AJ. "I honestly don't. It's not like there's anyone I can ask about it, not anyone with first-hand knowledge, that is. We're talking about something that happened, like, seventy-five years ago."

"Maybe," said his grandma. "But I know someone who can help answer that question — and so do you."

SaturDay MORNiNG

AJ crawled out of bed just before ten. It had taken him ages to get to sleep, what with the thoughts that swirled around in his brain and the buzzing of his phone. Steve had messaged him more than a million times, it seemed to AJ, reminding him about the rally at the school.

AJ got dressed and walked downstairs. "Good afternoon," his mom teased. "Grandma must have really tired you out with all her chores."

"I guess," said AJ. He was tired but not because he built a fence and cleaned out the chicken coop. "Where's Dad?"

"Some equipment broke at the mill. He's there right now dealing with it." AJ wasn't surprised. His dad had more than one hundred employees, but he often dealt with things himself. He was relieved his father was out. They hadn't spoken since their argument the previous day and AJ wasn't sure what he'd say if he saw his dad now.

"You want breakfast? I can whip you up some pancakes."

"No thanks," AJ said. "I'm not really hungry."

"Not hungry? That does not sound one bit like the Alex Sullivan Junior I know. Is everything all right?"

"I'm fine, Mom," AJ said. "I just don't feel like food right now."

"And you don't feel like talking to your friends, either?" she asked. "Steve phoned this morning while you were sleeping. Said he tried to reach you last night, but you didn't return any messages, which is another thing that doesn't sound like you, AJ."

"I forgot to charge my phone," said AJ. "That's all."

"Is that right?" His mom looked at her watch. "You have thirty minutes. You'd best get going — if you're going that is."

"They're expecting me to," AJ said. "Pretty much every kid from school's going to be there."

"Except for the kids from Big River First Nation," said his mom. His grandmother had said the same thing. "Is there anything you want to tell me?"

There were a million things AJ wanted to tell his mom. He wanted to tell her about his great-grandfather's prejudices. He wanted to tell her about Harold burning down the Freedom Camp, and more than anything to tell her what he'd discovered yesterday in an old dusty journal. A secret kept hidden for nearly seventy-five years. But somehow, he couldn't — at least not yet.

"No," he replied. "I have to get moving, Mom."

"AJ," his mom said before he left, "have you thought that it takes a lot of courage and integrity for Robert Thomas to do what he's doing? I love your dad, and I've known Buck Pearson my whole life but . . . " There was no need for her to finish the sentence.

"I know, Mom." AJ kissed his mom goodbye and within minutes was in his truck, heading down his driveway. Everyone was expecting him to be there: his best friend, all the town students, his dad. AJ had read Steve's messages. The news was going to be there as well. They were in town to cover Monday's school board meeting, and this was an exciting little bonus for them.

At the end of his driveway, AJ stopped. A left turn would take him to town and the rally. A right turn? That would lead him along the road to Big River First Nation, where his grandmother had suggested he might find the answer to the disturbing questions Harold's journal had raised. AJ sat there, his truck idling. His phone buzzed. It was Steve of course.

Rally starts in 15 minutes. We need u.

AJ felt like screaming. The easiest thing in the world was to turn left, go to the school, and stand in front of the gathered crowd to defend the reputation of his great-grandfather — and his own family in the process. It was the safest thing to do, the expected thing, the Sullivan thing.

Integrity. That was a Sullivan thing too.

"I can't believe I'm doing this," said AJ. He signalled right and pulled out of the driveway, tires kicking up dust as he drove north to Big River First Nation.

His phone rang. It was Steve calling. AJ ignored it. Two minutes later it rang again, and he ignored that call as well as he headed north. The first ten kilometres was a stretch of highway AJ knew well. After all, it led to the Sullivan

Sawmill. It took him less than ten minutes to reach the turn-off to the mill. He stopped. From the road he could see the sawmill, the planer building, the office, the piles of logs in the yard, waiting to be turned into the boards the mill churned out; wood that not only had built the town of Big River, but was shipped across the province, the country, and even the world itself. AJ also saw his dad's pickup in the parking lot.

His dad. He was not going to be happy. Then AJ's phone rang again. Steve, for the third time in five minutes. The rally was starting anytime now. AJ ignored it. His dad and his best friend were both expecting him to be there. There was a likelihood neither one of them would ever want to speak to him again after today.

AJ hit the gas. A minute or so later he had left the smooth pavement behind. For the next thirty kilometres he'd be travelling on gravel. AJ had never really thought about why the pavement ended at the mill, but now, he wondered if the reason was cost, an oversight, or something else entirely. There was no way the government would allow the residents of Big River to suffer this, AJ thought, but it didn't seem to bother them that the people from Big River First Nation had been driving the gravel highway for almost a century.

The forest closed in around the road, now a thin sliver of dirt. AJ's eyes darted instinctively from side to side, looking for movement in the ditches and the trees. It was something his dad had taught him from a young age. Spooked moose, deer, and sometimes even bears ran out onto the roads, and every year more than a couple of drivers hit one of them. These accidents usually ended in the death of the unfortunate animal, and sometimes that of the driver or the other occupants of the vehicle as well.

As he continued north, AJ saw nothing more than a few birds, however, and soon he reached the outskirts of the First Nation. It had been ages since AJ was last here. The community was only a short drive from town, but it was rare for residents of Big River to make the trip. There were about a thousand people who lived here. Big River First Nation had a large band office with a gym, a health centre with a nurse, a daycare, a police substation, outside basketball courts that doubled as a rink in the winter, and a small general store that sold the basics. For anything else, residents had to make the trip to town.

And then there was the church. The Big River First Nation church was called Our Lady of the River. It was well over a century old, AJ knew, built on a rise overlooking the river by Catholic missionaries who'd come up from the south in the 1880s. Beside the church was the old cemetery, wooden crosses, and grave markers visible behind the fence. The church was a provincial historic site and was well-known, with its white wooden exterior, tall steeple, and stained-glass windows. The windows had been shipped from Montreal, crossing the country by train, wagon, and riverboat, arriving at Big River packed carefully in straw-filled crates. AJ couldn't help thinking that it was too bad the authorities in his own century hadn't made the same sort of investment in the road to get here.

Like Big River, the First Nation was a working town. There were fields where cattle and horses grazed on the spring grass. There were a few old hay barns, wood faded with age. The houses on the First Nation were a mix of old and new, though no matter when they were built, they all looked as if the same person had designed them: basic boxes with adjacent sheds. Some houses had logging trucks and other equipment parked beside them, and like back in town, almost all the personal vehicles were pickup trucks or SUVs. This was not exactly car country.

While it had been a while since AJ was here, he remembered where he was going, though he had to admit he was nervous. AJ turned right and followed a driveway down to a house built above the river. There were a couple of familiar trucks parked in front of it, and AJ knew that people were at home. He parked, worked up his courage, walked to the door, and knocked.

"AJ Sullivan. I must admit I'm surprised to see you here," Robert Thomas said as he opened the door. "I would have thought you'd be at that thing at the school today."

"Hi, Mr. Thomas," AJ replied apprehensively.

"How can I help you?" Robert asked. He sounded somewhat wary, not that AJ could blame him for that.

There were a couple of things AJ wanted Mr. Thomas's help with, but there was something he needed to do first. "Is Jackson home?" he asked.

"What do you want?" It was Jackson who said it as he came to the front door. Jackson's face had been as banged up as AJ's. His lip was still swollen, and his right eye was still black and half-shut.

"I'm sorry." AJ knew he owed that much at least to his buddy. "I'm sorry I accused you, and I'm sorry I hit you. I shouldn't have done that."

"No shit," Jackson said angrily. "We've been friends since kindergarten."

"I know," AJ said.

"Ms. Shorthouse made you come out here and say that?" Jackson asked. He looked suspicious, to say the least.

"No," AJ replied. "I mean it. I was wrong."

"You look like crap," Jackson said.

"You got a couple of good hits in," AJ admitted. "I deserved them."

"You did deserve them," said Jackson. "Most people in town don't think so, though."

"I know." As far as pretty much every student who lived in town was concerned, AJ was a hero for hitting Jackson.

"Does your dad know you're out here, AJ?" Mr. Thomas asked. "I'm not very popular with him right now, and I don't think he'd be too pleased with you talking to me."

"He doesn't," said AJ. "And you're right about how he feels, but I need to talk to you."

"About what?" Instead of wary, Mr. Thomas now seemed curious.

"The Freedom Camp," said AJ, "specifically about a person who used to live there, a guy called James Antoine." That was the name AJ had read in Harold's journal and on the papers he'd found tucked within it. James Antoine would have known the truth of things and AJ hoped that he'd shared his story with someone else — someone Mr. Thomas would know.

Mr. Thomas looked shocked. "How do you know that name?"

"I found some of my great-grandfather's old journals,"

said AJ. "I read that James Antoine was one of the residents of the camp, that Harold burned down his house, and that maybe something terrible happened because of that. Do you know anything about what I'm talking about?"

"I do," Mr. Thomas said. "All too well."

"Can you tell me what happened, Mr. Thomas? What really happened the day Harold had the Freedom Camp burned down? The truth, no matter what it is."

"I could," said Mr. Thomas. "Or you can ask James Antoine himself. "He's still alive.""

Saturday Afternoon

"Alive?" AJ could hardly believe what he heard. "He must be a hundred years old!"

"One hundred and one, actually, but yes, James is still alive, and in quite good health. He lives just north of here, in a cabin off the river, and he may be old, but James is still sharp as a tack. Do you want to meet him?"

"Please." AJ was stunned. His grandma had told him to ask Mr. Thomas, but he had no idea whatsoever that James Antoine, the man whose life was changed all those years ago, was still alive. But maybe his grandma had, thought AJ. It wouldn't have surprised him at all if she had known all along. She'd lived in Big River her entire life and knew everything and everyone.

"We'll take my truck," said Mr. Thomas. Jackson and AJ hopped into Mr. Thomas's truck and soon they were bouncing down a narrow road that wound along the Big River. "James should be at home," Mr. Thomas said. "He doesn't get out much anymore, but he gets lots of visitors. People out here look after each other. Everyone knows James and we like to keep an eye on him, though James would be the first to deny he needed any help. He's very independent."

"Do you think he'll want to talk to me?" It was one thing that James Antoine was still alive, but quite another that he would want to talk to AJ, especially when he learned that AJ was Harold's descendant.

"I honestly don't know," said Mr. Thomas. "But if he does, I hope you're prepared to listen to what he'll say."

A few minutes north, Mr. Thomas turned off the main gravel road onto a small, rutted dirt track, so narrow that the bushes on either side leaned over and brushed against the truck as Mr. Thomas drove. The road followed the Big River, both snaking through the northern forest.

"You missing that 'save our school and statue rally' isn't going to sit well with your dad and the guys in town, AJ, you know that," said Jackson. "You're going to be more unpopular at school than me."

"I'm sure a lot of people are going to be pissed." AJ had resigned himself to that. He was glad that there was no cell service out at the Big River First Nation. Steve had been blowing up his phone back in town. AJ checked the time: 11:30. The rally at the school would be in full swing right now, hundreds of kids with signs, all demanding the school board refuse to remove the statue and change the school's name. It would not go unnoticed by anyone, students, townspeople, and out-of-town media alike, that Alex Sullivan Junior was absent. AJ almost felt sick at the consequences of disappointing his friends and his father. If this is what integrity looked like he wasn't sure he wanted any part of it.

"We're here." Mr. Thomas stopped the truck outside a small log cabin built in a clearing up the bank from the river, smoke puffing out of the round metal chimney. The cabin was old but just like the rest of the property, it was neat and tidy. AJ saw the familiar shapes of a smokehouse and a chicken coop. Looking at the coop he thought of his grandmother and felt a little better about things. His grandma was the only person in the world who understood just what he was trying to do. Everyone else in Big River may end up hating him, but at least she would stand by him, AJ knew.

An old Ford pickup truck was parked next to the cabin. "James still drives?" AJ asked.

"I told you he was independent," said Mr. Thomas as they got out of his truck. "James drives, and still likes hunting and fishing though he needs a little help these days."

Then the door of the cabin opened, and a man emerged. "Morning, James," Mr. Thomas said.

"This is a nice surprise, Robert," James Antoine said. AJ wasn't sure what he'd thought a more than one-hundred-year-old man would look like, but it wasn't this. James Antoine didn't seem any older than AJ's grandmother. "I wasn't expecting company this morning."

"It wasn't a planned visit," admitted Mr. Thomas, "but there's a young man from town who wants to talk to you."

"From town? He wants to talk to me?" James seemed completely taken aback. "Who?"

"Good morning, Mr. Antoine," AJ said nervously. "I have

a couple of questions if you don't mind."

"I don't think I know you, but you seem familiar," said James. The old man approached and studied AJ intently. "What's your name, son?"

"AJ — Alex, I mean," he said. "Alex Sullivan Junior."

"Sullivan? I know that name."

AJ felt incredibly uncomfortable but pressed on. "I believe you knew my great-grandfather. Harold Sullivan."

"Harold Sullivan." AJ could see a spark of recognition in James's eyes. "You look just like him. What does Harold's great-grandson want with me?"

"I found an old journal of Harold's," said AJ. "I read something in there about the day he had the Freedom Camp — your home — burned down. Something else happened that day, didn't it? Something that the people back in town don't know about, but they need to."

Pain flashed across James Antoine's face. "It was a long time ago. I'm not sure anyone wants to hear about it, especially people in town."

AJ understood exactly what James was saying. Up until a couple of days ago, he wouldn't have been willing to believe it himself. "All my life I grew up with Harold's legend," AJ said, "but I've learned some things about him over the last couple of days, and I need to know the truth, Mr. Antoine. The truth about Harold and that day."

"I'm sorry." James turned to head back to his cabin. "It was a long way to come for nothing. Have a good day, young man."

AJ had missed the rally, had fought with his father, and most likely had lost his best friend. This trip had cost him dearly, and AJ needed to know. "He wrote about the day he had your house burned down. Everything. In his own words," AJ repeated.

"Then you don't need to hear it from me," said the old man. "You know what happened."

"Mr. Antoine." AJ was desperate now. "You spoke to a police officer named Constable Tremblay. He took notes. I read them. I don't know how Harold ended up with them, but they were hidden in his journal. I know that the police didn't do anything about it. I'm not sure if you heard, sir, but there's going to be a meeting about taking down Harold's statue and renaming the school. This whole thing is tearing the town apart, and I need to know who my great-grandfather really was — and what he did."

James Antoine stood lost in thought for a moment, then slowly nodded. "The kettle's on. Come inside for a cup of tea."

The cabin was cozy and snug on the inside. A fire crackled within the pot-belly stove and the place was warm and smelled like woodsmoke. AJ, Jackson, and James Antoine sat around James's small table as Mr. Thomas poured tea, strong and black and sweetened with sugar.

"It was the winter of '43 when we shipped out to England," James said. "Me and a bunch of other guys from the reserve and town. I wasn't eighteen yet. We didn't have to sign up, but we did. Everyone knew Harold had volunteered again and if an old man near sixty was going to serve his country, there was no way us young guys were going to sit it out. Look at how young I was. Not much older than you."

There was a black and white photo of a very young James,

81

on the wall, smiling and in uniform. He stood next to a young woman. In his arms, he held a baby. "Sara and me, we were kids ourselves, but we'd just had our daughter Rose. She was hardly two months old when I enlisted. When I came back from Europe in the fall of '45 she was walking and talking. I missed the first two years of her life."

AJ sipped his tea, hanging on every word James said. He realized that this was the first time he'd spoken to a veteran of the Second World War. The war had ended almost eighty years ago. James could very well be the last remaining soldier who'd served in that conflict still alive in Big River, maybe one of the last in the province, even.

"Anyway, I get home and try to move on with my life and forget about the war," said James. "I was still a young man with a young family, and I got a job logging, but there wasn't enough housing on the reserve so Sara, Rose, and me lived with her parents for a spell. The Indian Agent tried to get more homes built, but there wasn't much money for my people and we didn't get the same benefits as the white soldiers."

AJ knew that. Mr. Corbett had taught them in Social Studies how First Nations veterans were treated differently. But that was stuff he'd learned in class. It sounded very different hearing about it from a person who had experienced it first-hand.

"We weren't the only ones in this situation," James said. "There were a couple of other veterans who were bunked in with their in-laws as well and by the spring of '47 with no help coming from Indian Affairs we'd had enough. Some of the guys had lost their status so they weren't even eligible to live on-reserve. They'd been away from home for four years. Somebody, I can't remember who, had the idea of building our own houses on the outskirts of town on a piece of land that used to belong to the reserve, but was taken by the government after the first war."

"I heard about that." AJ knew exactly what James was talking about. His own home was part of that land.

"We figured we'd spent the last couple of years fighting for freedom in Europe. It was the least the government could do, leave us alone and let us build our own homes. It's not like the land was being used, so we went ahead and did it. That's why we called it the Freedom Camp. We had fought for other people's freedom. We deserved some for ourselves"

"The newspaper called them squatter shacks," AJ said.

"That's what people said but it wasn't true," replied James. "We knew how to build things. Those houses were as good as anything in town and a darn bunch better than the places Indian Affairs usually built. We were happy and getting on with our lives. Until Harold Sullivan showed up."

For the next fifteen minutes, James Antoine spoke, confirming every awful detail AJ had read. AJ was transfixed, and though he already knew the details from the journal and the mysterious police notes, it was so much more real and tragic to hear it from the man who had actually experienced it.

"I am so sorry that happened," AJ said when the old man finished his story.

"I was too," James said. "Some of the things I'd seen and done in the war — they mess with a person, but I was dealing with it. For this to happen? It broke me." Even after so many years, AJ could see the pain etched deeply onto James's face, and he was heartbroken for him.

"Sara and me, we didn't last long afterward," James said. "I couldn't go back to her parents' place, and I drifted away, went down south to the city. They were tough years, lost years. I made some bad choices and was in a bad way. Was homeless, spent time in jail. I was lost for a long time until Robert's father found me and convinced me to come home." James Antoine's eyes glistened. "He was a good friend to me. He helped me straighten myself out, even gave me his old cabin. I've been here ever since."

AJ was teary but he didn't care. James's words, not just what happened the day Harold burned down his home, but the entire story had moved him more than anything he could remember. "Thank you," AJ said. "For sharing your story."

"You said there was some sort of meeting?" asked James.

"Yeah," AJ said. "The school board is going to hold a meeting about whether to remove my great-grandfather's statue and rename the high school. It's the fiftieth anniversary of Harold's death. My dad wants to create a scholarship in Harold's name, and it kind of set people off."

"People like me and my dad," Jackson said. "And AJ as well, it seems."

"This meeting," James began with an interest AJ wasn't expecting. "When is it?"

★ ★ ★

An hour later when AJ was back in cell service range, his phone lit up. Message after message popped up. There was voicemail as well, AJ saw though he didn't feel like pulling over to check. He knew who they were from. Steve, a bunch of other friends from school, his mom and dad; all wondering where he was probably — and why he didn't show up to a rally that was meant to protect the reputation of 'Hatchet' Harold, and the entire Sullivan family itself.

Integrity. Family. Community. Three of the four Sullivan words. Those words were great, AJ thought, but what if one came into conflict with another? After what AJ had learned over the past couple of days there was no way he could maintain his own integrity and defend a family member's actions, even if they happened many years ago.

AJ reached the driveway to the Home Ranch and felt a lump grow in his throat. His dad was already mad at him, and after today he was going to be furious, but before AJ could think about how he was going to deal with his father he saw a silver Chevy pickup driving toward him. AJ knew that truck. It was Steve Pearson. The two trucks stopped. Driver's side windows came down.

"AJ! Where the hell have you been? Your mom thought you were in a crash. I was about to go looking for you!"

"Sorry. There was something I had to do." AJ didn't feel like going into the details with Steve.

"Something you had to do?" Steve's voice went from relief to fury. "Something more important than showing up for your family, your school, and for me?"

"I'm sorry," AJ said. "I had to talk to Jackson."

"You had to talk to Jackson?" Steve sounded disgusted. "You had to go see that Indian asshole who started all this? I told everyone you'd be there, that you'd be speaking on behalf of all of us! And it is us, AJ. Us against them, and you chose

them. There were TV people there, AJ. They were looking to talk to you, and you weren't there!"

"Steve, it was just that — "

"I don't care what it was," snapped Steve. "You're an embarrassment to your family and your school, and you're no friend of mine. Not anymore." Steve sped away, his spinning tires kicking up gravel.

The greeting AJ received when he reached the house wasn't much better. "AJ! We were worried sick about you!" His mom ran out of the house as AJ parked his truck.

"I'm fine, Mom," he told her. "There was just something I had to do."

"Something more important than honouring your family?" It was if his father and Steve had rehearsed their lines together, AJ thought. "I know where you weren't," his dad said. "I want to know where you were."

"Big River First Nation. I had to speak to Jackson and his dad."

When AJ's father was angry, he yelled, but when he was furious his voice dropped almost to a whisper. It did so now. "You had to what?"

"There was something I had to find out," AJ said.

"What?" asked his mom. "What was so important you had to go and do that today of all times?"

"I found an old journal of Harold's," said AJ. "I read about something that happened at the Freedom Camp, something really bad, and I needed to find out so I — "

His father cut him off. "You needed to be at that school. That's what you needed to do. Your friends, your classmates, and this town needed you to be at that school and

86

you weren't."

"But, Dad," AJ protested. "You aren't listening to me. I found out something important."

"Nothing that happened more than seventy years ago is as important as sticking up for your family today, AJ."

"Alex," said AJ's mom, intervening. "Maybe you should hear what AJ was doing out there."

His father was having none of it. "It doesn't matter what he was doing. It's what he didn't do that counts, and he didn't stand up for his family when it counted." His voice was cold as winter snow. "You just make certain you show up to the board meeting on Monday. I'll be speaking on behalf of the family and the community, and you'll see how a Sullivan needs to act when his honour is on the line."

SUNDaY

AJ woke up early. Sometimes he liked to sleep in on Sundays, especially when he wasn't working at the mill or going fishing or heading to baseball practice, but this Sunday, even with nothing else to do, he found himself awake with the first rays of the rising sun.

His phone was turned off. The last thing AJ wanted to see was any messages from Steve Pearson or any of the other guys. His absence at the SOSS rally was big news, and just as AJ feared his no-show had upset a lot of people. AJ got dressed and headed downstairs to the kitchen. His mom and dad were still sleeping and for that he was grateful. The look on his father's face last night, and the tone of his voice had deeply upset AJ.

He didn't stand up for his family when it counted. Those words were like knives in AJ's heart. He worshipped his dad, and for

AJ's whole life, his entire identity had been intertwined with Harold's and the other members of the Sullivan family.

AJ didn't want to be around when his parents woke up and there was only one place he felt he could go. He shut the door quietly behind him and hopped in his truck. A little while later he arrived at his grandmother's house. She opened the door and stood on the porch as he pulled up, as if she had been expecting him.

"How did it go yesterday?" she asked.

"Did you know James Antoine?" AJ asked. "And did you know he was still alive?"

She nodded. "I knew James, and I suspected he was still around. I wasn't certain about it but if he was, I knew Robert would. Did you talk to him?"

"I did," said AJ. "He's a pretty amazing guy."

"And he told you what happened?"

"He did. Every word."

"Then come on in and have some breakfast," she said. "And tell me all about it."

An hour later AJ felt a bit better. He didn't realize he was hungry until he smelled the bacon Grandma cooked for him, and as he ate, he told her all about his visit to Big River First Nation and James Antoine's sad story. He also told her about the reception he'd received from both Steve and his father.

"I'm sorry about your friend, and I can imagine how your dad reacted," she said. "And you never told him what you found out?"

"I tried, Grandma, but he wasn't in any mood to listen. I'm a disappointment and a failure to him right now, and the entire town probably."

"Not to the entire town," she told him. "Not to James Antoine, not to Jackson and Robert Thomas, and certainly not to me. What you did took a lot of courage, Alex Junior."

"So now I'm a brave kid hated by the entire town, including my former best friend and my dad," AJ said. "I'm not sure it was worth it. I'll be lucky if I make it through school tomorrow without somebody killing me."

"You're not hated by everyone. And you will be just fine," she reassured him. "What are you going to do until then?"

"I don't know. Dig a hole and hide in it is what I want to do."

"You could do that," his grandmother said, "but there is something else you could do with your time, something that may help you put things in perspective."

AJ was surprised he hadn't thought of it already. The Freedom Camp and what happened there in September of 1949 was all AJ had been thinking about for days, but for some reason going to see the site for himself hadn't crossed his mind. He knew where James's house and the rest of the camp had been. Prospector Avenue, the northernmost residential street in Big River, was a dead end. There had been plans years ago to build more houses at the end of the street, but for some reason or the other those plans had fallen through, and the site of the Freedom Camp was now nothing but overgrown willows and pine trees.

AJ parked and stood at the end of the street. There was a trail that led into the bush. It was too close to town to be an animal trail, so it was probably made by kids, AJ reckoned. When AJ was younger, he and Steve and some of the other guys would create forts or simple treehouses in the woods around the Home Ranch, cutting trails through the trees to reach them. No doubt kids on Prospector Avenue had done the same. AJ followed the narrow trail and was soon surrounded by trees. He walked for a few minutes until a clearing appeared up ahead. It didn't take AJ long to realize that the clearing wasn't natural.

Although the forest had reclaimed much of the former site of the Freedom Camp, there was still evidence that James Antoine's house and five others once stood here. Boards, at one time pieces of lumber that had probably been cut at Sullivan Sawmills lay on the ground. They were more rot now than anything else, covered in moss and lichens. There were also scraps of metal: nails, old cans, and other artifacts. One piece of metal caught AJ's attention. He bent down to see what had once been an old bed frame, half-covered in ferns and brush. It was nothing but a twisted wreck, scorched black and partially melted from the heat of an inferno.

Suddenly AJ felt very sad. More than sad. It was if he could feel the pain that was caused here all those years ago, that the thing that happened here had left a memory held by the very land itself. Here he was, standing on the burned ruins of what had once been a home. James Antoine's, perhaps, or one of the other families', a home set to the torch, incinerated by AJ's own ancestor. More than just ruins, AJ knew as he looked at the clearing.

He realized what he needed to do. Although AJ risked losing his friends forever, and having his own dad disown him, as soon as he got home, he turned on his computer and got to work.

MoNDay

Going back to school on Monday morning was worse than AJ had imagined, and he'd imagined that it would be terrible. The security guards were still there, watching over the school and the statue, and a CBC TV news truck from down south was parked in the lot, getting set up to cover the school board meeting in the gym that evening.

AJ could see the tension on the faces of the kids from town and the kids from the First Nation. School felt uncomfortable and strange, and the worst thing of all was how the other kids from town reacted to him. "Where were you on Saturday?" "Why the hell didn't you show up?" and "We needed you," were the mild responses. The others ranged from anger to betrayal. Steve Pearson, AJ's best friend, a person he'd grown up with his entire life, wouldn't even acknowledge AJ except with a look of contempt.

Jackson wasn't at school. AJ spent lunch alone in the library working on his laptop, and when the bell rang he went to class, time passing agonizingly slow. Finally, the school day ended, but instead of going home, AJ made one quick stop and then headed to the town library. He still had more work to do.

★★★

When his phone read 6:45, AJ closed his laptop and drove back to the school. The board meeting to decide 'Hatchet' Harold's fate was only fifteen minutes away.

The parking lot was already nearly full. AJ saw his dad's truck. Steve Pearson was there already as well, and so was his grandmother and Mr. Thomas and a couple of hundred other people. This meeting promised to be the most attended school board meeting in Big River history, and certainly the only one that was making national news.

AJ entered the gym. Rows and rows of chairs were full of people. On the stage at the front of the gym sat the school board and Dr. Gwynn, the district superintendent. They all looked nervous, and AJ could only imagine what was going through their minds.

His parents and grandmother were in the third row, and one look was all it took for AJ to realize just how seriously his dad was taking this meeting. His father was wearing new jeans, his cowboy boots were clean, and he had on a suit jacket and a tie. AJ could count on one hand the number of times he'd seen his dad wearing a tie, and that was at weddings or funerals. His father also had a handful of paper, his neat handwriting covering the pages with the speech that he'd been working on — the speech that would defend the family honour.

"You're here," said his dad. "I wasn't sure you'd make it. Thought maybe you had something more important to do."

"Nope," said AJ, ignoring his dad's tone as he sat down. "Nothing more important than this."

"Well, that's good," said his dad, voice slightly softer. "It will go a long way making things right with Steve."

The Pearsons, Steve, Buck, and his mom Annie, sat a few rows behind the Sullivan family. AJ looked at Steve and could still see the anger on his face. And on Buck's face, too. Buck had been called out by Robert as well, and AJ had done nothing about it.

His phone buzzed. AJ looked down and read the message. "Son, put that thing away and pay attention," said his dad. "This is going to be a very important day in the history of this town."

The crowd was a near-even mix of Big River town and Big River First Nation. Several reporters were there: radio, newspaper, and of course the TV station, who had their cameras set up to film the board; Dr. Gwynn, and the people who would line up to plead their case. The police were there as well, several constables as well as Staff Sergeant Murdoch, the officer in charge of the Big River detachment. This was a big event, and AJ was certain the last thing she wanted was a protest that got out of hand in front of a TV camera. Right now, everyone was calm and respectful, but as recent events had shown, things could turn on a dime.

Julie Sandusky was the chair of the school board, and she

called the meeting to order. Ms. Sandusky's son Nick played on the baseball team with AJ. They were friends — at least they *were* friends, AJ thought. Nick had helped Steve organize the SOSS rally, and AJ knew what Nick thought about renaming the school.

"Thank you all for coming," said Ms. Sandusky. "As you know we are here to have a very difficult conversation, and I thank you all in advance for remaining civil and respectful of everyone's opinions — even if you don't agree with them." Dr. Gwynn nodded in agreement, but he looked as if he wanted to be anywhere in the world but on that stage in front of the assembled crowd.

Remaining civil. That was the proper thing to say, AJ knew, though it was probably little more than wishful thinking. A while ago in English class, AJ had learned the expression *powder keg.* That was a pretty good definition of what was going on in Big River. He felt as if the whole town could blow up at any time.

"We have had many requests from the public to speak on the issue before us: the petition to rename Sullivan High School and to remove the statue of Harold Sullivan from the front of the school."

"Ridiculous!" shouted somebody in the crowd.

"Tear it down!" said a voice.

"Save our school and statue!" somebody else cried. AJ was pretty sure it was Steve. There were a lot of students in the audience, and most were wearing Sullivan High School colours.

"As I said before, we will remain civil and respectful to all opinions or else you'll be asked to leave. And that includes you, Steve Pearson," she said, confirming AJ's guess. Ms. Sandusky wasn't the kind of person to get pushed around by anyone, AJ knew. The Sanduskys had been in Big River almost as long as the Sullivans, and everyone respected them, but even Julie Sandusky was going to have a tough time managing this crowd.

"Our first speaker is Alex Sullivan," said Ms. Sandusky, and Alex's dad started to his feet until Ms. Sandusky added, "Alex Sullivan Junior, that is."

"*You're* speaking?" AJ's father seemed very surprised.

"I am," AJ told him as he got to his feet, computer bag in his hands, and his legs wobbling with nerves. "I stopped by the board office after school and asked to be put on the list."

AJ walked slowly up to the mic that was set up by the stage. There was a table next to the mic. He took out his computer, hooked it up to the projector, and soon Harold Sullivan's face, the face from the famous picture of Harold and his hatchet glowed on the screen. At the sight of Harold, some people in the crowd cheered, others booed, but all were very interested in what AJ had to say.

"My name is AJ Sullivan," he began. "Alex Sullivan Junior. Harold Sullivan was my great-grandfather." AJ looked out into the sea of faces in the gym, faces he'd known his entire life. "Since I was a little boy, I've been proud of my family and my heritage. Harold Sullivan was an important person in this community for a lot of years." As AJ spoke, he clicked on the handheld presentation mouse he'd borrowed from Ms. Wallace in the library.

"Harold fought for this country in two wars," said AJ, as more images of Harold appeared. The young officer from the first war and the older, tired-looking major from the second. "Harold's mill hired more people than any other business in town," he continued as picture after picture flashed on the screen. "He was a businessman and a politician. Harold Sullivan was a very important figure in the history of Big River and his name and legacy are still important here, almost fifty years after he died. As recent events have shown."

There was applause from the residents of Big River though everyone from the First Nation was silent. AJ paused and looked at his father. He was smiling and looking on at AJ with approval, but AJ was certain that look was about to change with what he was about to say next. "But there was another side to Harold. I learned he discriminated against Indigenous people. He worked hard to make sure kids from Big River First Nation didn't go to school in town and that they attend Sturgeon Lake Residential School instead. Harold was not a perfect person. There were many people who were prejudiced against First Nations people back then, and my great-grandfather was one of them, both in his actions and words."

AJ's father's expression was now unreadable as he stared at his son. AJ looked to his grandmother, sitting next to his mom, and while AJ could only guess at what his father was thinking, he could read the pride written all over his grandmother's face.

"In September of 1949, when Harold was mayor of Big River, he had several homes on the outskirts of town burned down. He called the people squatters, called their homes an eyesore, but the people who lived there called this place the Freedom Camp. They were from Big River First Nation, veterans of the Second World War and their families, and they had no other place to go. The government was building homes for white veterans but not Indigenous ones, so they built homes themselves. And on the day Harold and some other men from town came to burn down the Freedom Camp, something very sad happened."

AJ looked into the crowd and saw Robert and Jackson Thomas. And one other person he knew as well. "But that is not my story to tell. That story belongs to James Antoine, the last living survivor of the Freedom Camp."

★★★

There was a buzz of curiosity in the crowd as James, with Robert and Jackson Thomas walking beside him, made his way to the microphone. "You sure about this, Mr. Antoine?" asked AJ. He'd doubted that the old man was going to be there, let alone speak until Jackson had texted AJ, confirming both.

"Yes," James said as he turned and leaned into the mic. James was shorter than AJ by a good six inches, and AJ had to bend the mic over so James could reach it.

"I'm sorry, Mr. Antoine, but you're not on the speakers' list." It was Mr. Herdman, one of the school board members. "We have a process we need to follow. Those are the rules. Perhaps if there is time after the registered speakers have had their turn you can say something."

"You go right ahead, sir." Ms. Sandusky was the chair of the board, and there was no way she was going to turn James Antoine away, not on a matter of this much importance and certainly not with over one hundred members of the Big River First Nation in attendance.

"Thank you, Ms. Sandusky," said AJ. Mr. Herdman sat down with a sour look on his face but didn't protest.

"My name is James Antoine," the old man began, his voice surprisingly clear. James started his story the same way he had with AJ back at his cabin, picking it up in 1943 when he shipped off to England, and though AJ knew exactly where the story was going, he hung on every word, just like all the other people in the gym.

"Then I heard the cars arrive," said James. "My wife Sara and I thought it was the Indian Agent. It was September, and Rose was six, and she was supposed to go to the Sturgeon Lake School, but I wasn't going to let them take her away. Too many bad things happened at that school. I told Rose to run inside and hide, and not come out no matter what. But it wasn't the Indian Agent. It was Harold Sullivan and some guys from town, including a police officer. Harold told me that we'd been squatting on town land long enough. We'd been warned and that he was going to burn our houses down."

No matter what side of the statue argument they were on, everybody in the gym was completely silent. "We tried to argue but they wouldn't listen to us. Harold wouldn't even let anyone go in and get any of our things. He said we'd had plenty of chances to heed the warning. Then this guy, he approaches my house with a can of gas. Sara's screaming and crying because Rose is inside hiding. I tell them to wait and let me get my daughter out of the house, but they didn't let me. Thought I was going to get a gun or trick them or something, I figure. I begged Harold to go in and get her himself then. I don't think he believed me either, but he went in anyway. He came out a couple of minutes later by himself, said he looked everywhere but he didn't see anyone, called me a liar, said I was stalling for time.

"Then Harold took the can of gas, splashed it on the walls, and set the place on fire. I was fighting to get free; it took three of those guys to hold me back. Sara was crying. I was screaming and trying to fight to get into that house and rescue Rose, but I couldn't. I watched as the house went up like a candle. Had been a dry summer that year. Soon my house and all the other houses were burning. I remember feeling the heat of the flames on my face. Even then I kept trying to get free to run in and find Rose and maybe I would have until the police officer jumped on top of me and put me in handcuffs.

"All that flame and smoke, I could only watch, helpless, as the place burned. Hope she didn't suffer too much. That's what I think about, how scared she would have been. Only took a couple of minutes and the whole place looked like some of the houses I'd seen in France, burned up by the fighting. Except this wasn't the war. This was my home. I told her not to come out, under any circumstances. She listened. And she died because of it. Because of me."

James took a minute, collecting his thoughts in the silent gymnasium. "They put me in the town jail for a week afterward. I'd assaulted those men, they said. While I was in the cell, I told the police officer my daughter was in the house. He took notes, said he'd look into it. Couple days later he said they searched through the ashes when the place was cool enough, but they didn't find a trace of her. Couldn't say I was surprised about that. Fire had burned so hot, there was nothing left of her. He told me maybe she'd run away. One policeman said I probably didn't have a daughter in the first place. Eventually they let me out of the cell, said that they were giving me a break, and not going to charge me if I didn't cause any more trouble. And if I kept my mouth shut."

"It's true," AJ said. "I found Harold's journal. He wrote about that day — and he knew what he had done." AJ clicked the mouse and a page from Harold's diary appeared.

"At first, I thought that Antoine fellow was lying about his child hiding somewhere inside." AJ read Harold's words out loud, following the small, neat cursive writing line by line. *"But there was something in his voice, in how he and his wife wailed as their shack burned down, and even as it burned, I feared I had done a most terrible thing, that I set their house on fire with their young child still inside, and that her blood is on my hands."*

"The constable who investigated was named Peter Tremblay," AJ said. "He was a young man who'd served in the army. He'd have known who Harold was and the influence he had. Like Harold, I think Constable Tremblay also knew that Rose Antoine had died in the fire. He interviewed Harold about it, as well as James Antoine."

AJ clicked on the mouse again, and one of the loose pages that had been tucked in Harold's journal appeared. "I can't say for sure how Harold ended up with Constable Tremblay's interview notes, but my guess is that they both knew the truth, that they had been part of a great tragedy, and the best thing for them, and for Big River as well, was to keep it quiet and pretend it never happened. After all, who would believe James Antoine over '*Hatchet*' Harold Sullivan?

"But Harold knew," said AJ. "He wrote about that day several more times in his journal, just as he wrote about his own daughter who he'd lost, way back in World War One. She was just a couple of years old when she died. Harold was overseas in France, and he never even met her, but her death really tore him up. I think he understood how James felt, more than anyone could possibly know. His actions and his words never really changed, but I think that maybe the guilt tore him up inside."

AJ put his arm around James's frail shoulders, his heart swelling with admiration and respect. For a man past one hundred years old to speak so eloquently, so passionately, it had brought AJ and many other people in the gym to tears.

"All my life I grew up believing that Harold was a hero and that he built the town I know and love. And I think that is still true," AJ added, "but I've also learned that there were things about my great-grandfather that were neither heroic nor good. It's not my decision to make, and I understand that there will be people opposed to it, but I believe that Mr. Thomas's petition to have the school renamed and the statue removed is the right thing to do. I also don't believe that my dad's scholarship should bear Harold's name either."

AJ looked at Ms. Sandusky and then stared into the audience at his family. His mom and his grandmother were crying. His father's eyes glistened as well, and there was a look on his face that AJ wasn't sure he'd ever see again. The revelations were very hard on his father, AJ could tell. But he also knew his dad was proud of him. "Doing the right thing isn't easy sometimes," AJ said. "But that doesn't mean we don't do it. Not if we have integrity."

Saturday Morning

AJ Sullivan and Jackson Thomas stood on the remnants of the Freedom Camp. They'd brought with them a bouquet of marigolds and had placed them on the ground where James Antoine's house had once stood. AJ didn't know the first thing about flowers, but the marigolds were orange, and both boys thought that was very appropriate.

"I hope you're doing okay, wherever you are, Rose," AJ said.

"She is," Jackson assured him. "She's with her mom and her ancestors, and they're looking after her."

"That sounds pretty good," AJ said.

"I gotta say I'm still shocked your dad stood up after you and spoke in favour of renaming the school and taking down the statue," Jackson said.

"Not as shocked as Buck and Steve Pearson," AJ said. People had mostly stayed silent after he'd talked, probably more shocked and surprised than anything else, but when Alex Sullivan Senior himself stood up and agreed with AJ's request, that pretty much killed any opposition to the petition, except from the Pearson men, who said a few choice words before they left the meeting.

There were more than a few threatening messages from Steve on AJ's phone after that. Now it was like AJ didn't exist to Steve, and some of the other boys as well. It hurt, AJ admitted. The Pearsons and the Sullivans had been friends for more than a century. "They'll get over it," AJ's dad had said. AJ hoped so, but even if they didn't, there was nothing he could do.

"It's also kind of cool that your dad is going to keep funding the scholarship but call it the Rose Antoine Memorial," said Jackson. "That went over pretty well with everyone back home. I thought your dad was tough as nails, but he didn't look that way at the board meeting, not after hearing James speak."

"He said he wasn't crying, it was just allergies," said AJ, but he didn't believe that.

"Do you know when the school board going to announce the new name of the school?" asked Jackson.

"They're going to ask for people's opinions and come up with something by September, I think," AJ said. "At least that's what Ms. Shorthouse said when I asked."

"What about Harold Sullivan's statue? Is it going to stay at your house forever?"

The fate of 'Hatchet' Harold's statue was the talk of the town. Most people agreed it should be moved from the school, but that was where agreement ended. Some wanted it displayed someplace else while others wanted it burned down. The school board wasn't sure what to do with it until somebody looked in the district archives and realized that AJ's grandfather had paid for it and lent it to the school, which made the statue Sullivan property, and a Sullivan problem. That was why 'Hatchet' Harold's statue was currently sitting in the barn at the Home Ranch.

"My dad isn't sure what the heck to do with it," AJ said, "but my grandmother has an idea. She suggested it come to her place and she would keep it in the chicken coop."

"The chicken coop? Are you serious?" asked Jackson.

"A hundred percent serious," AJ replied. "Harold liked chickens."

" 'Hatchet' Harold Sullivan liked chickens? You're kidding me," said Jackson.

"No, it's true," said AJ. "My grandmother swears it. And more than that," he added, "apparently they liked him back."

ACKNOWLEDGEMENTS

I would like to thank Jim Lorimer and Lorimer Publishing for their unwavering support and encouragement through ten years and seven books. A special thanks goes to Allister Thompson and Megan Blythe for their editorial prowess and support of this project. My thanks as always to my wife Sharon for her boundless love and support. Finally, I would like to recognize and thank everyone in Canada who, in the name of truth and reconciliation, sees wrongs and works hard to set them right.

AUthoR'S Note

When I began to write this book, I was at first thinking of events in my home province of British Columbia. Events in the news and from my own life, growing up in a small northern town very similar to Big River, helped inspire it. But there are places like Big River and people Like AJ, Jackson, and Steve across the country.

School Statue Showdown is a work of fiction, but the historical events referenced in this story are true. Land was cut off from reservations to give to returning white soldiers. In fact, in both World Wars Indigenous veterans were not given the same rights and opportunities upon their return, and many Indigenous soldiers, all of whom volunteered to fight, lost their Indigenous status. This was because of the Indian Act (see: https://www.thecanadianencyclopedia.ca/en/timeline/the-indian-act) a piece of law created in 1876 that is still in effect today and still called the same thing. I don't reference the act directly in this book, but the Indian Act hangs over every page of this story. Over the years, the Indian Act has been used to discriminate against and assimilate Indigenous people. While it protects certain rights, its main purpose has been to control Indigenous people. Over the years, the Indian Act has done things like made it illegal for Indigenous people to work as doctors, lawyers, or other professionals, to leave their reserves, or to attend university.

Furthermore, legislation meant to reward soldiers returning from war such as the Soldier Settlement Act led to the government confiscating tens of thousands of acres from reserves to provide land for non-Indigenous soldiers (see: https://www.thecanadianencyclopedia.ca/en/article/indigenous-peoples-and-the-first-world-war).

Like AJ, Harold Sullivan is fictional, but there were men like Harold all across this country. One such person was Alan Webster Neill from Port Alberni, BC, and my story is heavily influenced by the events of Neill's life and the decision to remove his name from a school. In a time span of more than sixty years, Neill served as a municipal, provincial, and federal politician. Even in his own time, he was known to hold extreme racist views against Indigenous people and Asian Canadians (see: https://www.thecanadianencyclopedia.ca/en/article/segregation-of-asian-canadians). He supported residential schools and once said that his role was to stand for a "white British Columbia." Neill even had a covenant on the property title of his house that prevented any Asians, except for servants, from living there. In 2018, three high school students discovered the covenant was still on title. They were the ones who petitioned to have it removed.

In 2021, after much debate, controversy, and opposition, the school was renamed Tsuma-as, which means "Little creek running all over the ground" in the Nuu-chah-nulth language (see: https://www.cbc.ca/news/canada/british-columbia/port-alberni-elementary-school-renaming-tsuma-as-1.6194305). I was also really surprised to learn that while Neill's name has been removed from the school, there is still a street named after him in Port Alberni.

There are other examples of opposition to renaming schools in BC. In 2020, the Prince George School District decided to rename the recently rebuilt Kelly Road Secondary School, a school named after a local pioneer, to Shas-Ti, which means "Grizzly Bear Path" in the Dakelh language. The name change was fought vigorously by members of the community, with many taking to social media to vent their anger (see: https://www.cbc.ca/news/canada/british-columbia/kelly-road-shas-ti-secondary-school-prince-george-bc-re-naming-1.5548744). The Facebook posts are not pleasant reading and are still online. Ultimately, the district decided to keep the old name and add the new one. This compromise did little to please people on both sides of the issue.

Both Harold Sullivan and Alan Webster Neill worked as Indian agents, a position that lasted from the 1870s to the 1960s in Canada. The role of an Indian agent was to enforce the Canadian government's policy of assimilation on reserves (see: https://www.thecanadianencyclopedia.ca/en/article/indian-agents-in-canada). Their power over Indigenous people was enormous. Until World War Two, an Indigenous person needed a pass from an Indian agent to leave their reserve, and they could be arrested if found off-reserve without one. Indian agents, as well as the police, were also key in ensuring Indigenous children were taken to residential schools (see: https://www.thecanadianencyclopedia.ca/en/timeline/residential-schools) and Indian agents.

The lack of an investigation over the events at Freedom Camp is also inspired by real events. Over the years, police in Canada, including the RCMP, have been accused of not treating crimes against Indigenous people seriously, of covering up such crimes and even participating in them. And as far as the Freedom Camp itself?

In 1968, in Fort St. James, BC, a local priest name 24

Camp succeeded in destroying the 24 Camp, a similarly named "squatters camp" built not on town land but on property belonging to the church. The newspaper article in this book is almost entirely based on a story about the destruction of the camp from an August 1968 article in the Nechako Chronicle newspaper. I wasn't born when this happened, but I remember hearing about it as a child. Even little things like the pavement ending at the sawmill are based on real situations. There are examples all around British Columbia and Canada where this happens. It was certainly the case in my hometown that for years the asphalt ended well before reaching the Tl'azt'en Nation north of town.

The image of Hatchet Harold's statue covered in orange paint and vandalized is based on real events. The statue of Egerton Ryerson, the namesake of what used to be Ryerson University and is now Toronto Metropolitan University, suffered this fate (see: https://www.thecanadianencyclopedia.ca/en/article/egerton-ryerson), and the city of Victoria, where John A. Macdonald once served as an MP, has removed his statue. Schools in Calgary and Ontario have dropped the PM's name and adopted new ones, and the city of Victoria as removed its statue of Macdonald from public display. But not without fierce protest. I was not surprised when researching this book that the issue of renaming schools and other public places is not without controversy and opposition. A 2020 Leger survey found that the majority of Canadians did not support the renaming of schools, buildings, and streets or the removal of statues.

So where does that leave Big River, Big River First Nation, and AJ Sullivan? Where does it leave you and I? How do we judge public figures with complicated pasts, people who have done great things, but are also responsible for injustice and great harm? How does Canada honour the Calls to Action from the Truth and Reconciliation Commission (see: https://www.thecanadianencyclopedia.ca/en/article/truth-and-reconciliation-commission) and move forward in a mutually respectful relationship with Indigenous peoples? I believe the answer to that begins with education. We can't commit to meaningful reconciliation with Indigenous communities and with our own past until we have the courage to learn the truth about those pasts. I see this book as one way to begin that journey.